GW00703519

MICHAEL BUTTERWORTH

X Marks the Spot.

A Symphony in Black in Four Movements

COLLINS, ST JAMES'S PLACE, LONDON

William Collins Sons & Co Ltd
London · Glasgow · Sydney · Auckland
Toronto · Johannesburg

First published 1978
© Michael Butterworth, 1978

ISBN 0 00 231934 9

Set in Intertype Boskerville
Made and printed in Great Britain by
William Collins Sons & Co Ltd Glasgow

For Julian More

Scherzo and Trio

I

IF EDGAR FERNWORTHY had not lingered in the square at Ravello on account of a young woman's breasts, there is no telling how his life might have ended. As it was, he ordered another Campari-soda and shifted his chair the better to make shy glances in her direction. She and her boy-friend, or husband, had just arrived in the square in a VW beetle with German number plates. Ash-blonde, pink and peeling, she wore a check cotton shirt with no brassière under. She sat down, crossed her legs, volubly addressed her male companion, undid another button of her shirt, unselfconsciously dabbed the damp upper slopes of her breasts with a spotted handkerchief. And changed Fernworthy's life.

Minutes later (the ice in his second Campari had scarcely lost its shape) a giant touring bus laboured up the winding road from Amalfi, and wheeled to a stop with a gusting of air-brakes. A stream of tourists poured out, cameras already cocked, dark shades panning round the square. The guide or courier was an intense little woman in Bermuda shorts. She corralled her charges by the shiny great side of the bus and said :

'All right, this is Ravello. You got the Palazzo Rudolfo, that's with the garden which gave Richard Wagner the situation for Parsifal's Home of the Flower Maidens. Also the Villa Cimbrone, with really great views; this is where Marconi stayed, also the Duke of Windsor. But first you got the Duomo San Pantaleone and the Liquefaction of the Blood. This way, okay?'

Patiently, they followed her and straggled up the steps towards the central, open door of the church. Torn between necessity and tender lust, Fernworthy downed the rest of his drink, cast a glance at the German girl's attributes, and joined on the end of the line of tourists, who were too good to miss.

Inside the church, it was crypt-cool and green from the light of the dusty windows. A sacristan in a rusty soutane and a two-day stubble was shepherding the party towards a low door on the left of the altar. Fernworthy took advantage of a tendency for some of them to wander out of line and look around the place to move forward and slot himself in behind a stout man in an alpaca jacket – a manoeuvre that did not pass unobserved by a male child of about seven years whose place might with some justification be said to have been usurped.

'Maw, this old man's snuck in here!' His shrill cry of martyrdom echoed from the barrel vault above. The man in the alpaca jacket turned round and met Fernworthy eye-to-eye, seeking recognition and finding none.

'Great country they got here,' said the man.

'Mmmm,' agreed Fernworthy.

They filed past the pulpit, which Fernworthy, not being an admirer of the basilican type of church, had always thought to be the best thing in the building : resting on marble columns and intricately carved wild beasts – one of the finest pieces of Cosmati work in Southern Italy, in his opinion. Nearing the door, the line became more bunched; the advance a swinging lock-step, closely pressed. Someone hacked at Fernworthy's ankle, and he turned and looked down into the malevolent face of the small boy.

'Pardon me,' said the boy piously.

'You're welcome,' was Fernworthy's mild response.

The door led into a semi-circular apse, and the line of people were passing through it and out of a door at the other end, pausing on the way to gaze in through a barred window immediately behind the altar, from which issued a muted, rosy light which gave their faces a look of being bathed in hellfire. The advance was slow. Fernworthy kept close behind the stout man in the alpaca jacket, so close that he could smell the other's after-shave. The small boy had vanished into the gloom below waist level. They came, at length, to the barred window, Fernworthy and the stout man, side-by-side. There, in a locked and bolted rectangular compartment about the size of a picnic hamper, a small family refrigerator, or an office safe, stood an antique-looking bottle of dull, cut glass, like a trendy perfume flask. It was part-filled with some material, the top layer of which looked like grease. There was a silting of sediment at the bottom. The middle section – which was pierced by the light from a red electric bulb positioned behind – seemed the colour and consistency of bottled coffee essence.

'The Liquefaction,' murmured a woman somewhere off on Fernworthy's left, 'the true Liquefaction of the Blood is not due for some weeks yet.'

Fernworthy swung his hip, gingerly, to probe the buttock of the man in the alpaca jacket, and located a swelling there. He experienced his habitual flutter of stage fright, and countered it by taking a couple of deep breaths. In – pause, one, two, three – out. And then repeat.

'Well, now, that's really something!' said Fernworthy's victim, as the former delicately lifted up the skirt of the alpaca jacket, permitting the fingers of his right hand to slide smoothly into the pants' hip pocket and close upon

– his heart gave a leap for triumph – *real crocodile!* He made the withdrawal : it was beautifully done.

'Maw! This old guy's swiped Mr O'Flynn's billfold!'

Fernworthy dropped his haul – always the best policy, for possession is nine points of guilt – and elbowed his way swiftly towards the far door.

'Pardon me,' he said. 'Do you mind? Thank you. I feel rather faint. The heat . . .'

'Stop, thief!' came the shriek of that monstrous child.

'Get a hold of that guy!'

Fernworthy won his way out of the door and came face to face with a sacristan, who held out to him a small black bag on the end of a rod.

'*Grazie, signor. Grazie.*'

'I'm not of your persuasion,' muttered Fernworthy. 'But, though a Fundamentalist, I found it very impressive. Do you mind? Thank you.'

He slid past the affronted sacristan, and raced down the aisle just as the hue and cry really got under way. Out into the sudden sunlight, his eyes were dazzled. It would be fair to say that he negotiated the dozen or so steps down into the square by sheer good luck. His good luck gave out half-way across the open space, when he ran under the wheels of a passing ambulance, was knocked unconscious, and suffered multiple compound fractures and extensive lacerations of his hand. His right, working hand.

The ambulance was on its way to Amalfi hospital, so they took the injured man along with them – there being no protests from the horrified posse, and Mr O'Flynn having recovered his property, anyhow.

At the hospital, in an operating theatre overlooking the glory of the Gulf of Sorrento, the duty surgeon toyed briefly with the notion of patching up Fernworthy's hand, in the slender hope of re-establishing it, with nature's help, as a viable appendage; but the limpid blue light of the Gulf reflected from the ceiling, and an awareness of the young nursing nun beside him, her plump roundness delineated under her theatre gown, moved him to obscure philosophies. A brief moment of carnal pleasure was followed, in the surgeon's mind, by a sad revelation of mortality. With a sigh, he severed what remained of Fernworthy's hand and dropped it into the foot-bin.

THAT WAS IN June. August found Fernworthy back in London and drawing what people of his age and class still mistakenly refer to as 'National Assistance'; that is, £10.90 a week as an unmarried householder, plus £8.00 a week for rent. Prompted by a kindly clerk at his local office of Health and Social Security, he had also applied for a disability pension, on the grounds of having lost his hand as the result of an industrial accident. And in this assertion, Fernworthy was not so much lying as continuing a lifelong self-deceit.

His passport read: Profession, Artist-Painter. His new records at the Health and Social Security office stated: Fernworthy, E.A.; Occupation – artist (disabled). All his adult life, he had acted, dressed, dreamed, thought like an artist. In fact, he was a passably good draughtsman in the steely manner of the Vorticist Wyndham Lewis, and had twice been accepted by the Royal Academy summer exhibitions; but he seldom touched brush or pen because an instinct for perfectionism, quite unmatched to his abilities, made work a misery. So he contented himself by living the role of the artist-painter, and it was in this role that he had lost his hand in Italy. In an industrial accident.

No one in the world knew that, ever since he came down from Cambridge in 1950, Fernworthy had made his full-time living – and a very good living – as a common pickpocket. It was a competence he had picked up at school, in company with a boy named Arthur Ealing; the two of them had practised the mode of instruction devised by Fagin in *Oliver Twist* and had soon been able to remove articles of trivia from the pockets of their schoolfellows, graduating to more solid properties of their masters, and eventually to selected citizens of the town. When Fernworthy was eighteen, the sudden death of his father would have precluded his entry to Trinity College, had not the proceeds of his secret craft been more than enough to see him through in considerable style. Arthur Ealing was killed in a flying accident a year after leaving school (in his own aircraft – bought out of what must be described as other people's pockets), so that – till the disaster in Ravello – Fernworthy's secret had been known to himself alone. And now, as a result of that disaster, it might almost be said as a result of his mild addiction to the female breast, he had been deprived, in one stroke of a surgeon's scalpel, of both a livelihood and an illusion. For Fernworthy had been strongly right-handed : he could neither draw nor 'dip' with his left.

A Friday afternoon in mid-August found him in the common waiting-room at his local office of Health and Social Security – where, all unknowing, he was to have his second brush with the machinations of blind fate.

It was steamy-hot and smelling of institutional antiseptic. The walls were painted green to waist level and brown all below. A motley collection of people sat in rows of hard-backed chairs that fronted an alcove with doors leading off to right and left, where notices said : *To cubicles A and B*, and *To Cubicles C and D*. Another notice made a plaintive – and disregarded – suggestion that it would be appreciated if the clientele did not smoke.

'Mrs Ducane to Cubicle A,' was announced through a loudspeaker on the wall behind Fernworthy. Whoever it was omitted to switch off, so he heard the voice continue, *sotto voce* : 'She's a Mrs the way I'm a bloody opera singer.' Happily, this went unheard by the lady in question, who was busily assembling children to the number of three; an infant in arms, one in a perambulator pushed by the third. And young Mrs Ducane, tall, blonde and incredibly thin in a semi-transparent khaftan worn over nothing but knickers, was palpably pregnant yet again.

'Good luck in there, honey,' said the young man on Fernworthy's left, who had the air of being the surrogate Mr Ducane. The remark was ignored by the tall blonde, who was shepherding her offspring before her. It occurred to Fernworthy to wonder why she did not leave them with the father.

The man was grinning at him, showing very white teeth. He wore a T-shirt emblazoned with the arms of Oxford University.

'Were you "up"?' asked Fernworthy, nodding at his companion's chest.

'Hell, no,' replied the other amiably. 'I'm not the stuff that Rhodes scholars are made of.'

'Canadian?'

'American. Coker's my name. James J. Coker, but my pals call me "Jay".' He extended a beefy paw to Fernworthy, glanced down in puzzlement when it was not met, and grimaced to see the stump of wrist with its new, pink skin and the sutures still covered with Band-Aid. 'Jesus, what happened to you?'

'I met with an accident in Italy,' explained Fernworthy. 'While working.' He gave Coker his left hand. It was something else he was going to have to get used to.

'Working in Italy, huh? Some kind of construction work, or an oilman, maybe?' He glanced doubtfully at Fernworthy's velvet jacket, the floppy bow tie in the manner of the 'thirties Bohemian.

'I am an artist,' said Fernworthy simply. 'That's to say,

I *was* an artist.'

'Hell, that's a tough break,' said Jay Coker.

They lapsed into silence. Faintly over the loudspeaker came the dialogue between Mrs Ducane and the clerk in Cubicle A.

'Mrs Ducane, you say that the TV rental people are threatening to recover their set because you're three months in arrears. But, Mrs Ducane, I don't appear to have any record of your being a party to this rental transaction. Ah! – Mrs Ducane, will you kindly restrain that child from overturning my Out Tray?'

There came the sound of a slap, followed by an anguished howl, which, being presently reduced to a keening whine, provided a background to all that followed.

'*You'll* have to pay the rental. I know my rights. Shut up, Floyd! Will you shut up!'

'But, Mrs Ducane, you must realize that the Department can't make itself responsible for rental transactions that you make *after* becoming a recipient of . . . will you please not let that other child crawl around my feet? Now it's trying to take off my Hush Puppies!'

'Come here, Warren, you little bugger!'

Jay Coker nudged Fernworthy. 'Got a great way with kids, has Eunice,' he said, jerking his head towards the loudspeaker.

'I gather that,' said Fernworthy.

'Some Mau-Mau, huh. She'll get what she's after. I'd lay you two to one, but it'd be a sin to take your dough.'

'I can well believe it,' said Fernworthy.

'This country of yours,' said Coker. 'Now I'm a great believer in free enterprise, self-sufficiency, you name it. When Nixon referred to the likes of you and me as "bums on relief", he was stating a basic truth. Yes, sir, a basic truth. But this country of yours – here you have a way of working the welfare state so it doesn't hurt. Know what I mean? Take Soviet Russia. Now, in Soviet Russia, do you imagine that them moujiks in Moscow have hand-outs for the asking? No, sir! All they got are the mummified bodies of Marx and Lenin on show – that and a load of promises.'

The dialogue between the clerks and Mrs Ducane had by now been submerged in the cries of all three children.

Presently, Fernworthy said : 'Lenin. Only Lenin.'

'Pardon me?'

'Only Lenin is on public view in Moscow,' said Fernworthy. 'Karl Marx is buried in Highgate.'

'Highgate? This is some suburb of Moscow, maybe. So I won't quibble. They got Lenin on show in Red Square, they got Marx buried at Highgate. And a whole heap of promises.'

'Highgate is in North London,' said Fernworthy. 'He's buried in the cemetery there.'

Coker looked hard and long at his companion, and said : 'You are putting me on.'

'No, honestly. Karl Marx died in London – at least, I assume he died in London – and was buried in Highgate Cemetery.'

'We are both speaking of the same guy? Karl Marx – founder of Communism? Lot of hair and a beard?'

'That's right.'

'Buried in North London, England?'

'Yes.'

Jay Coker exhaled loudly. Smote his brow with the palm of his hand. 'Now I heard everything!' he exclaimed. 'You are telling me that this country – which is still a capitalistic country, and a monarchy moreover – gives refuge to the remains of the arch-revolutionary of modern times? I find this ironical, not to say paradoxical. These remains – they are guarded, night and day, by the British Army, no doubt, to protect their resting place from defacement by the displaced thousands who have taken refuge in Britain from the Communist regimes of Poland, Czechoslovakia, Hungary, etcetera, not to mention Russia itself.'

There was a crackle from the loudspeaker, as someone went to switch it on and found it to be on already.

'Mr Fernworthy to Cubicle C.'

Fernworthy nodded to his new friend and went out through the door on the right of the alcove. The clerk in Cubicle C enjoyed dealing with gentlefolk down on their luck through no fault of their own.

'Sorry about the application for the disability pension, Mr Fernworthy. Still under consideration. Can you call back Thursday? Might have some news then.'

'Of course. Thank you.'

'No other problems?'

'No, everything's fine, thanks. Unless . . .'

'Yes, Mr Fernworthy?'

'I know this sounds rather absurd, but – do you happen to know if we – that is, the Government – make any provision to guard the grave of Karl Marx?'

The clerk gave him a sharp glance; sniffed the air, as if trying to detect strong spirits. 'I've really no idea,' he said. 'It isn't our department. That would come under the Home Office.'

'Of course. Sorry to have bothered you.'

'No bother, Mr Fernworthy. Good afternoon.'

'Good afternoon. And thank you.'

He came out of the alcove on the heels of Mrs Ducane, who was shepherding her riotous offspring before her with the look of a woman who had got her own way – an impression that she confirmed by giving a V-sign to the waiting Coker. The American got up – revealing that

he was a big man, well over six feet and massively built
— and put an arm round her shoulders, ruffled the hair
of the oldest child. Fernworthy nodded farewell to Coker
on the way past, and was surprised when the American
made some excuse to his consort and came trotting
athletically after him.

'Hey, feller. As regards what we were saying . . .'

'About Karl Marx?'

'Sure. I was asking you . . .'

'If the grave was guarded or anything.'

'That's right.'

'Are you doing anything this afternoon, Mr Coker?'

'Call me Jay. Hell, no — I'm as free as air.'

'Let's go to Highgate and see for ourselves.'

When they came out of the underground station at the
bottom of Highgate Hill, the sky was dark to the north
and threatening rain.

'Which way, Ed?' demanded Coker.

'It has to be at the top of the hill,' said Fernworthy.
'Let's walk up there and ask the first intelligent-looking
native we meet.'

There was lightning and a thunderclap from almost
immediately overhead when they came to the hospital
half-way up the hill. A stream of caped and coiffed
nurses ran, shrieking, across the road as the rain came
in a sudden flurry. It was soon over; but threatening
again when they came in sight of an elderly priest.

Coker said : 'Here's a guy who should know.'

Fernworthy stopped, and asked : 'Father, could you
direct us, please, to Highgate Cemetery?'

Shrewd eyes glittered behind pebbled lenses. 'Ah, it's
your Karl Marx, is it?'

'He's the chap we're after, Father,' admitted Fernworthy sheepishly.

'Well now,' said the other, pointing with his furled umbrella. 'You turn left at the church, cross Waterlow Park diagonally, and your cemetery's right there.'

'Thanks, Father. We'll give your kind regards to Karl Marx.'

'You believe that, you'll believe anything,' grinned the old priest.

At the top of the hill, another flash and crash brought the rain bucketing down, and they ran for the shelter of the church porch; stood there, watching the rain rebounding knee high on the gravelled drive. Faintly, through the opened door behind them, came the smell of incense.

'You a Catholic, Ed?' asked Coker.

'I'm a strong supporter of the team,' said Fernworthy. 'The Catholic Church has a lot going for it. Spells and smells. It's the mystery, you know. The Protestants turned their backs on the mystery, and nowadays seem largely to concern themselves with dispensing tea and buns. I'll back a saintly relic with well-authenticated miraculous properties against tea and buns, any day of the week.' And to his mind came the recollection of the dark apse of San Pantaleone. He shuddered.

'I guess, in the long run, it's gonna win out against Communism,' said Coker.

'It's an even bet,' said Fernworthy. 'As you said earlier, Jay, they've nothing going for them but Lenin's mummified body and a load of promises. Even by that simplistic yardstick, the Catholics are winning at a sharp trot. Their promises are both more extravagant and more specific, and, despite what the Humanists say, are quite impervious to logic. In the area of relics, the disparity is laughable. Against Lenin's mummy in Red Square can be set a mountain of sacred bits and pieces spread all over the world, from Glasgow to Santiago de Com-

postela, from the duomo of San Pantaleone at Ravello – '
here he winced – 'to Guadalupe, San Salvador, and the
Relics of New Spain.

'Jawbones and thighbones, bottles of blood that
liquefy on the dot every year; eye teeth and snippets of
scalp, whole skeletons seated in the glory of beaten silver
and embedded gems; mummified hands, hearts sealed in
lead capsules, sufficient pieces of the True Cross to build
another bridge across the River Kwai.

'Nothing – not Karl Marx and all his works; not the
Red Army, Navy and Air Force; or the smug content-
ment of British Labour life-peers as they stare down the
length of jumbo cigars through the windows of chauffeur-
driven limousines upon the undeserving proletariat –
none of these things can prevail, in the end, against the
great groundswell of simple faith that's generated by the
religious hardware I've described. Why, my dear fellow,
the sheer intrinsic value of all this mass of stuff, were it
to be auctioned at Sotheby's and Christies, would provide
enough to eclipse the total revenue of the Soviet bloc,
and pay to equip a latter-day Christian crusade with
sufficient armaments to win Armageddon.'

'You don't say!' cried Coker. 'So there's big dough in
religious relics?'

'Not any longer,' said Fernworthy. 'Not in a big way,
as in former days. What dealers in the antique trade
would describe as "the real flash stuff" – the saints' jawbones of impressive provenance, blood that demonstrably
liquefies – all that sort of religious merchandise has
reached its centre of gravity, its permanent abode, in the
major ecclesiastical institutions of the world and will
never come on the market again. All that remains is the
small change: Jordan water, Lourdes water, rosaries
blessed by the Pope, and everything down into the area
of coloured picture postcards of Mount Carmel. If you

have ambitions to get into the relics game, old man, you're a few centuries too late for the big pickings.'

Another roll of thunder sounded above Highgate Hill. Coker thrust his huge hands more deeply into the pockets of his Levis and stared glumly at the rain.

'Do they charge admission to see Lenin's mummy?' he asked at length. 'I've seen movie shots of these folks standing in line right across Red Square. Some take for the box office.'

'I don't know,' said Fernworthy. 'I imagine it's free, but I really don't know. But they could charge a big admission, and it would scarcely deter a good Communist who's, say, made a pilgrimage all the way from Omsk or Tomsk, to gaze upon their number two saint.'

'And the more so, if our guy from Omsk or Tomsk could see the big feller himself,' said Coker. 'Man, a double-feature would pull in the customers, would it not? I wonder the Soviets don't negotiate a deal with the British for Marx's remains in exchange for two or three battleships.'

'A few thousand million credit in good hard currency would be more acceptable here,' said Fernworthy tartly.

Coker said : 'While not wishing unduly to depress you, Ed, it seems likely to me that the Soviets figure all they have to do it sit around and let history work in their favour. And then they'll have all of Western Europe – with Karl Marx as a bonus.'

'I expect you're right,' said Fernworthy. 'I expect they'll have him in Red Square in the end.'

'It would be kind of nice,' said Coker, 'to anticipate that happy event – with some incidental financial benefit to oneself and friends.'

Their eyes met.

Fernworthy said : 'Pinch Karl Marx and sell him to the Russians? It would be amusing to examine the possibility of carrying out such a feat.'

'Strictly for the laughs.'

'An academic exercise. A dry run, if you like.'

'I have to tell you, Ed. In the area of respect for the dead, I got plenny scruples.'

'One's religious scruples,' said Fernworthy, 'would scarcely be at risk with the subject under discussion. And in the matter of respect for the dead, what more deferential act than to transport the subject from this contaminated soil? Soil that has been watered by the tears of the proletariat . . .'

'And is still being watered,' interposed Coker. 'As we have heard this afternoon, this land still rings with the cries of little children and the anguished pleading of their poor mothers.'

'Quite so,' agreed Fernworthy. 'What better than to transport him to the proletarian paradise that was his own brain child? To the flat-capped Arcadia, Nirvana beyond the Neva.'

'Man, that would be like doing him a favour,' said Coker.

The rain ceased as suddenly as it had begun. They walked quickly through the park, past neat flowerbeds with dahlias lined up like guardsmen, a lake, an aviary with noisy macaws, an old lady in a plastic pixie hood feeding an icecream cone to a Pekingese, a park-keeper stabbing up sweet papers and used contraceptives with a pin on a stick. The cemetery gates were alongside the exit from the park.

'It looks a pretty big area,' said Fernworthy. 'Do we ask someone to direct us to the grave?'

'In view of our new involvement with the subject in question,' said Coker. 'And though we are playing it strictly for laughs, I would suggest a more oblique and cautious approach.'

They searched – and found. Fernworthy recognized the grave from illustrations : a massive iron portrait head of Marx set atop a squat stone block. Even from afar, it looked a formidable proposition.

'Forget it,' said Coker. 'Nothing less than a portable crane is gonna shift that monument. No, sir !'

At close quarters, due to a disproportion between the head and its support, the monument appeared to shrink in size, but remained formidable.

' *"Workers of all lands unite"*,' read Coker, and went on : ' *"The philosophers have only interpreted the world in various ways. The point however is to change it."* Well, I guess you could say he did that, all right !'

There was another, longer inscription in smaller lettering, set in the middle of the block.

> Jenny von Westphalen
> The beloved wife of Karl Marx
> Born 12 February 1814
> Died 2nd December 1881
>
> And Karl Marx
> Born May 5th 1818
> Died March 14th 1883
>
> And Harry Longuet
> Their grandson
> Born July 4th 1878
> Died March 20th 1883
>
> And Helena Demuth
> Born Jan 1st 1823
> Died Nov 4th 1890

And Eleanor Marx
Daughter of Karl Marx
Born Jan 16th 1855
Died March 31 1898

'I had no idea!' cried Fernworthy, dismayed. 'And I'm sure it's not generally known that there are no less than four other people buried here with Marx. And three of them, you see, are later interments.'

Coker said: 'This means that to reach him you first have either to haul off that monument – or tunnel underneath it. Then you likely have to move out three coffins to get to the jackpot. Ed, I can't tell you how gratified I am that we have only been playing this idea along for the laughs. And yet . . .'

'Yes, Jay?'

'I was just thinking,' said Coker. 'Let's say Marx is worth a million pounds, call it two million dollars, to the Soviets. So you have two million bucks stashed away under that little old hunk of stone and iron. As a job of work it does not compare with breaking into a bank and making off with the contents of the safe deposit vault – a feat which, as we know, is regularly performed all over the world. I would say, Ed, that a job like the one we see before us is not in the same league. Compared with the real thing, this would be like breaking into a kid's piggybank.'

'There *must* be a way to do it!' cried Fernworthy.

Coker looked at his watch. 'It is nearly five-thirty o'clock,' he said. 'By the time we get back down the hill the licensing laws of this sceptered isle will permit the opening of the public houses. I invite you to join me in a few jars of beer, over which we will examine the problem in some depth.'

'But strictly for the laughs.'

'As you say.'

Setting off back along the path towards the exit gates, they saw a gang of three workmen mark out a six foot by three foot space and start digging. Without any comment, Fernworthy quickened his pace and Coker slowed his, so that they passed the diggers and went out of the cemetery separately. It seemed the natural thing to do.

III

THE WHOLE enterprise might have foundered there, but for their choice of pub, which was dictated by the sudden return of the rain. They ran the last few steps to a beckoning doorway, and plunged in, laughing and slapping the wetness from their sleeves and shoulders. It was a large and gloomy Victorian pub, heavily overlaid with up-to-date ticky-tacky. There was no one there but a barman in a Union Jack T-shirt.

'What are you going to have, Ed?'

'No, this is on me, Jay. I brought you on this wild goose chase.'

'Well, I'll have a pint of best bitter. Hell, it's been fun anyhow, and we haven't finished our deliberations yet.'

They took their drinks – beer for Coker and a gin-and-mixed for Fernworthy – over to the far end of the bar-room, facing a low stage upon which stood an upright piano. They need not have bothered about withdrawing themselves in secrecy; the barman switched on taped beat music, through which their ensuing conversation was carried.

'Here's to you, Ed.'

'Your very good health, Jay,' said Fernworthy. 'And to the memory of you-know-who.' And, when they had drunk: 'Now, to our deliberations. You say that head-stone couldn't be shifted without a crane?'

The big American shook his head. 'Uh-huh. You got the block of stone and the head on top. Call that eight tons, maybe more. For that you're gonna need a crane in the fifteen-, twenty-ton range. Man, that's a piece of hardware you can't drive around the streets without attracting some notice.'

'There's no question of being able to do it in daylight,' mused Fernworthy. 'What do you think to getting it in there at night? According to the notices at the gates, they close weekdays at five in the summer – ' he consulted his pocket diary, in which he had scribbled a few lines – 'except for Bank Holiday Monday, when they close at four.'

'The extra hour of daylight, now that's going to be of no aid at all,' said Coker. 'Your operating time's gonna be between, say, eleven at night till dawn. At this time of the year, call it six hours. Make it five hours for safety. In this time, you have to drive a twenty-ton crane from wherever you parked it out of sight, force the gates, haul off the headstone. And all without being seen or heard. And don't forget there's a hospital just over the cemetery wall. A lot of folks are awake in a hospital nights – and most of 'em mighty sensitive to noise.'

'I think a night crane job is out,' said Fernworthy.

'I, too, am inclined to that belief, Ed,' said Coker. 'And likewise at daytime, unless by some kind of trick – like we posed as authorized persons conducting an exhumation.'

'A trick? It's worth thinking about. But not now. Let's go through the remaining options. You mentioned tunnelling.'

'From where I am standing now,' said Coker, 'I see tunnelling at night as the only option. But it's not attractive. To name but a few – ' he ticked off the points on his big, stubby fingers – 'It's dark. You have th whole weight of the headstone above you, which wou dispose the earth to fall in and bury you alongside Ma and his friends. This hole you're digging is gonna be a size to permit the removal of a coffin, or what's left of a coffin.'

'Perhaps four coffins,' said Fernworthy. 'Remembering that there were three interments after Marx, it might be necessary first to bring out the three on top of him.'

Coker said : 'Add to that, you don't know – and you won't know till you get in there – if the coffins are simply piled one above the other, or in two piles. All this you're gonna have to learn while you're doing the job.'

'It sounds pretty hopeless,' said Fernworthy, draining his glass. 'For, in addition to all that, you have the task of positively identifying which is Marx.'

'I would say in many regards that that will be the simplest part,' said Coker. 'Down there, you got five skeletons and whatever remains of five coffins. However they are disposed, one of the skeletons, and one alone, is that of an adult male. Anyone with a fair knowledge of anatomy could identify Marx at a glance. Do you want another drink?'

'Please, Jay. Same again.'

While Coker was up at the bar counter, Fernworthy gazed gloomily about him. The pub was beginning to fill up with the first of the Friday night trade : mostly middle-aged couples of urban proletarian mould; local folk who all knew each other and greeted one another by name. The womenfolk were mostly stout and given to outbursts of eldritch laughter; the men cloth-capped, shrewd-eyed, taciturn. They all drank sitting down, the glasses set on the tables before them.

On the wall at the back of the stage was a hand-written poster that announced a feast of entertainment for the night in question. One was promised : Delicious Sheila Dazzle in her strip extraordinary; everybody's favourite dragster Esmé von Berlin; and the Baffling Zoltan, conjurer supreme. And commencing at 9 p.m.

Fernworthy glanced at his watch : six forty-five. However protracted their deliberations, there did not seem to be enough material, sufficient options, to keep them there till nine o'clock. Blessedly, they would be out before the commencement of the cabaret.

Coker returned with the drinks. He had bought himself a long thin cigar, which he had stuck at a sharp angle in the corner of his mouth in a manner that reminded Fernworthy of the illustrations of Captain Kettle in the bound volumes of *Pearson's Magazine* that had so delighted his youth.

'I am thinking,' said Coker, 'that night-tunnelling is riddled with snags, know what I mean?'

Fernworthy nodded. 'There's no doubt about it : the best option is to lift off the headstone by crane and sort out the contents of the grave at leisure.'

'So you might as well ask for the moon.'

'Or – we contrive it, as you suggested, by some kind of trick. Quite openly. With folks looking on and accepting our *bona fides* unquestioningly. Perhaps even with the police holding back the crowds of curious onlookers. And a police motorcycle escort when we drive away with what we came for.'

'I like it,' said Coker. 'That method has style.'

'Also very unlikely,' said Fernworthy, gazing sadly into his drink.

Highly unlikely – the whole enterprise. But curiously satisfying to contemplate. Call it a million pounds. Half share in a million pounds – that was something to think about, faced, as one was, with the prospect of a lifetime on National Assistance and Social Security. A poor substitute, that, for the freedom and comparative affluence that his – 'former discipline' was how he always referred to it in his own mind – that his former discipline had brought him. To maintain anything like a standard of civilized living, to be able to travel abroad, for instance, he would soon have to sell some of the treasured pictures and bibelots that were his whole life, and upon which he had invested his every spare penny. The Louis Quinze snuff boxes, the Victorian tear-bottle, the undoubted Meissonnier drawing of the dragoon, the early Sickert, the Minton bullfighter. All those and the rest would have to go. And beyond that – emptiness. Institutionalized old age as a resentful pensioner of a faceless state system. Never again to walk among the triumphant fountains of the Villa D'Este, or see the first light of dawn from the Rialto bridge, with the sounds of the market people on the quays below; never again to wander in the Prado, or stand in the great light of *The Burial of Count Orgaz*.

He roused himself . . .

'Laying aside the question of how we shall work this greatly to be desired trick,' he said, 'tell me about yourself, Jay. How long have you been over here?'

'Coming up to a year,' replied the other. 'I had a six-month work permit that expired last March. If I could raise the fare and something extra to have made it all worth while, I might even go back and tell the folks in Milwaukee that it's all been simply divine fun. The way it is with me now, they'll all know I blew it the way I blew medical school.'

'You studied to be a doctor?' asked Fernworthy, interested. 'That's why you were able to make the point about identifying you-know-who.'

'Sure. I blew out on physiology and biochemistry, but I scraped by on anatomy. Gimme half an hour with a text-book, and I'd have the characteristics of a male adult skeleton right here at my fingertips. Yes, sir.'

Fernworthy took a long swallow of his gin-and-mixed. He was beginning to feel quite tipsy, he decided. 'Do you know, Jay?' he said. 'Considering the nature of the

enterprise under discussion, it really is quite a remarkable coincidence that you should possess this very necessary qualification. Quite remarkable. But please continue.
You failed your exams and had to leave medical
school...'

'Football, that was my downfall,' said Coker. 'So
when the smart guys were back there in the laboratory,
I'm out on the field doing great things. All right. I'm
out. So I get this yen to make some distance between
me and the folks at home, so I lit out for England with
this six-month work permit. Six months, I work on
motorway construction as a crane driver...'

Their eyes met.

'Did you say – *crane driver*?' breathed Fernworthy.

'Yeah. And, you know – like, I never gave it a thought.
It only just hit me!'

'It's written in the stars,' said Fernworthy in an awed
voice. 'That you and I should meet. And that our conversation should have taken the turn it did.' He seized his
companion by the arm. 'This convinces me, Jay. I'm not
a superstitious man, but I tell you – it was pre-ordained.
We're going to get him out of that grave, my friend.
And we're going to sell him for a million!'

The deliberations had turned into something of a pre-
mature celebration party for two. Two hours and four
gins-and-mixed later, Fernworthy was telling his new
friend of his fears for the future (happily now allayed by
the undoubted success of their forthcoming enterprise),
of his pictures and bibelots that graced his two-roomed,
self-contained flat in St John's Wood. He touched upon
his mother and father, both deceased. Growing ever
more lacrymose he spoke of the best friend of his life
so far: that same Arthur Ealing with whom he had
developed the 'discipline'. He did not mention the

discipline. He expressed the hope, now verging on a certainty, that Jay Coker would take the place of that departed comrade. Glassy-eyed and swaying in his seat from the effects of six pints of best bitter, Coker echoed the hope that this would indeed be so, and added his conviction that Fernworthy had already supplanted in his affections one Arthur R. Wright, who had been his blood-brother in high school.

At nine o'clock, a smiling young man in a blond toupee briskly took his seat at the piano on the stage and started to play a medley of old-time favourites, in which the clientele of the public bar joined by singing such words as they could recall and la-la-ing the remainder. The cabaret had begun.

Fernworthy closed his eyes. When he opened them, he was gazing upon a young and heavily made-up female who, without any suggestion upon his part, was standing before him removing her brassière. A lifelong celibate whose only direct sexual adventure had been an embarrassingly fruitless visit to a prostitute in Florence, Fernworthy's familiarity with the undraped female form was limited – apart from manifestations of the genre in the plastic arts – to one visit to the *Folies Bergère*, which he had not greatly enjoyed, and his accidental intrusion upon a beach in the South of France where certain extremes of undress were tolerated – were even mandatory. The latter episode, Fernworthy could only bring himself to recall with horror : having indignantly refused to remove his shirt, let alone his trousers and underwear, he had been chased from the beach by a posse of muscular, mother-naked Frenchmen.

Heavy-eyed, but manifestly interested, he focused his unsteady gaze upon the antics of the young ecdysiast. Really, he thought, there was much to commend it. He should not have thrown in the sponge so easily. Of course, he had always known his predilections : a well-filled blouse had always had the power to attract him. There had been the girl in the square at Ravello – no, not to think of that!

Perhaps it was not too late to try again.

If one's fortunes improved . . .

The next time he opened his eyes, the place of the young woman had been taken by a spry, balding creature in a seedy evening dress suit, who was pulling yard upon yard of multi-coloured chiffon from a paper cone, to the noisy appreciation of his audience. Fernworthy's flickering eyelids were arrested by the advent of the conjuror's assistant – who was none other than the young ecdysiast, now clad in a shiny, cheap dress, with her ample bosom girt high like a pouter pigeon. She smiled directly at Fernworthy and he smiled back.

'And now, ladies and gents,' said the conjuror. 'A trick that will set you all wondering. Yes, lady, you'll be able to try it on the old man when you get to bed tonight. What's that? I'm glad I didn't hear that! Where was I? A pack of cards. Brand new. Tear off the seal. Give it to my beautiful assistant to pass round the front row. How are you tonight, Sheila darling? Tickle your ass with a feather. Don't hit me – all I said was "particularly nasty weather", haha! That's right, darling, show the gentleman in the front there. Just riffle through the pack, sir, and assure yourself they're all there.'

The girl came down from the stage and handed the pack of cards to Fernworthy. Close up, she smelt of sweat and talcum powder. Underneath the pancake make-up, her face was unformed and wary; childishness overlaid with experience. She could not have been a day over seventeen.

'Go on, shuffle through the bloody things!' she hissed to Fernworthy crossly. 'Can't stand 'ere all bloody night!'

Clumsily, he riffled through the pack, and would have dropped the lot, but for her intervention. And when she leaned forward to contain them in his clumsy grasp, he looked into the deep, damp, pink cleft of her bosom.

'Satisfied with the cards, sir?' cried the conjurer.

'Er – yes,' replied Fernworthy.

'Fifty-two are there – four different suits?'

'Yes – I – I think so. Just counting them . . .'

'Don't bloody bother!' hissed his tormentress, snatching them from him and flashing him a false smile. She handed them up to her principal.

'Complete pack of fifty-two cards,' said the conjurer, shuffling them with devastating expertise. 'I will now deal four cards right off the top of the pack on to the table. One, two, three, four. Lay the pack aside. Now – I would like a lady in the audience to call out the name of a card. Any card. Yes? You, madam? Speak up. Can't hear you, love.'

'Ace of Spades!' A female voice from somewhere behind Fernworthy's head.

'Ace of Spades!' cried the conjurer. 'Four cards on the table. I cry Sim-salabim! Pick up the card nearest to me. IT'S THE ACE OF SPADES! Thank you, thank you!'

Much applause, in which Fernworthy joined. Glancing to his companion, he saw that Coker was apparently asleep. The girl ecdysiast smothered a yawn.

'Ace of Spades removed,' said the conjurer. 'Leaves the possibility of the remaining three cards being any three of the fifty-one cards still in the pack. One thing we can be sure of – none of 'em's going to be the Ace of Spades. Ain't that right, lady? But – here! Wait a minute!' He snatched up the three cards in swift succession, holding them up for all to see. 'What have we got here? ANOTHER ACE OF SPADES! AND ANOTHER! AND ANOTHER! Thank you, thank you. That completes my performance for this evening, ladies and gentlemen. A big hand for my charming young assistant. Thank you.'

Coker stirred himself, yawned and sat up. 'That sure as hell is the worst card trick I ever did see,' he declared.

'I thought it was rather neat,' said Fernworthy, gazing wistfully after the retreating back of the young ecdysiast. Yes, he really must revise his ideas. It wasn't too late. Forty-nine was no age at all nowadays . . .

'Do me a favour!' cried Coker. 'This guy palms the four aces and deals 'em out on the table. All he has to do then is rely upon his plant in the audience to stay sober enough to call out the card he needs. Omygawd! Don't tell me we now have a drag act!'

The young man in the blond toupee had taken his place again at the piano and was playing 'The Stripper' with a lot of pedal. On to the stage stalked a tall figure in a glittering sequined sheath and a picture hat. Plucked eyebrows. A blue chin.

'Do you mind if we go, old man?' asked Fernworthy. 'I'm feeling rather sick as a matter of fact.'

'Man, that's just fine by me,' declared Coker.

Together, they rose and walked unsteadily towards the door. Their places were immediately taken by the two who had been sitting behind them. To the strains of 'The Stripper', the vision in sequins removed one long glove with a promise of protracted dalliance . . .

Outside, it had stopped raining. Fernworthy leaned against a lamp-post, retched. Felt better.

'It's been a delightful evening, Jay,' he said. 'Even though we didn't arrive at a conclusion.'

'One thing's for sure,' said Coker. 'We're gonna make it, Ed. Like you said : "It's written in the stars." '

They both looked up as one. The sky above London N19 was swept clear of clouds and all ablaze. The ragged W of the constellation of Cassiopeia commended itself to James J. Coker. He pointed.

'There's our sign, Ed boy !' he cried. 'Turn it upside down, and it's an M – and M stands for Marx !'

'Edgar Aetheling Fernworthy, you stand accused of feloniously removing the body of the late Karl Marx from its undoubted resting place, and this to the detriment of the Queen's peace. How do you plead, Edgar Aetheling Fernworthy? Are you Guilty or Not Guilty . . .?'

Fernworthy shuddered and threw up into the lavatory pan, pulled the chain, dabbed his lips. Washing himself in the hand basin, he thought, it really has been a quite astonishing day. And the curious thing was that, drunk as he had been, and sober as he now undoubtedly was, the image – the idea – of going through with the enterprise was still as hard and positive as it had been at the moment when he had had the inspiration that his partnership with Jay Coker had possessed a pre-ordained quality.

He and Coker had parted company in a tube train : the American for Kilburn, where he lived with the very pregnant Mrs Eunice Ducane and her children (Fernworthy had not probed his new friend about that particular *ménage*, nor had Coker vouchsafed any information), and he for St John's Wood. They had exchanged addresses, naturally, and had planned to meet – the unemployed and state-assisted being free to make such assignations as the spirit moves them, where and when –

in the National Gallery the following afternoon at three.

Yes, a quite remarkable day. The beginning – inauspicious (he had spent the morning at the launderette); the afternoon – inspired; the night – banal. His mind went back to the girl stripper. Decidedly, he must make a late entry into the sexual stakes. Money opens all doors, even the portals of hymen. He giggled at the gentle vulgarity and spread some toothpaste on his brush. Decidedly, she had looked better nude than dressed and in the company of that incredibly bad and vulgar low comedian posing as a conjuror. Jay Coker had been right, of course : the card trick in which he himself had played such an ignominious small part was quite the worst ever. The palming of the four cards, the accomplice in the audience. So simple really. Like the famous tale of Columbus's egg : the proposition absurd; the solution a cheat.

(How to stand an egg on its pointed end? Simply give it a sharp tap on the table top and make a slight dent in the shell. It will stand.)

THE TRICK . . . !

And now the tap was gushing, and the overflow had become gorged on the continuing onrush of water, so that the basin was filled and the water splattering upon the bathroom floor about his feet, soaking his carpet slippers, lifting the furry bath mat and making of it a raft in a small sea, soon lapping about his ankles and threatening to rise above the small dam at the door and engulf the entire flat and the one below. And all the time, Fernworthy was staring, uncaring, at his reflection in the mirror, with his hand and arm and loaded toothbrush poised an inch from his open mouth. Entranced.

Presently, he found the voice to utter . . .

'Eureka!'

Next, in frenzied alarm, he pulled out the plug of the basin and turned off the tap. The tenant below him – a middle-aged lady Civil Servant of forbidding mien and savage disposition – was of such a quality as to drive out all other considerations save those of emergency. Frantic with anxiety, he raced to fetch a bucket and mop from his narrow kitchen, and with them he slopped up all the spilt water in his bathroom. And all the time singing the joyful paeon in his heart :

'That's the trick! Like the conjurer's! Like old Columbus's – a cheat. But specifically more like the conjurer's cheat. Now you see it, now you don't! It's gone – it's still there!

'YIPPEEEE![2]

IV

'MADEMOISELLE, *un grand verre d'absinthe avec un tout petit soupçon d'eau.*'

'*Voilà, monsieur.*'

'*Merci. Vous êtes bien jolie. Si nous couchons ensemble . . .*'

'*Monsieur, vous êtes insupportable!*'

Fernworthy stood before Manet's 'Bar at the *Folies Bergère*' and addressed this imaginary conversation to the pretty blonde with the wide open, cow's eyes that stared eternally from out of the soundless bustle of the great room. It was far and away his favourite picture, and the girl his favourite girl. He many times thought that he would die for the pleasure of being able to step into the picture and be with her for ever; and was immersed in this particular conceit when Coker came into the gallery and sighted him.

The big American was in shirtsleeves, and carried a thick book under his arm. He winked at Fernworthy.

'Are we still in business, partner?' he asked.

'More than ever,' asserted Fernworthy. 'Come over here and sit down. I've some tremendous news for you.'

They took their places side by side on one of the sofas. A crocodile of young schoolgirls filed past, and they eyed Coker, one after another.

When they were alone again, the American asked: 'Well, what's this news, Ed?'

'I've thought of how to do the trick!' cried Fernworthy.

'You mean . . .?'

'How to raise you-know-who in full view of everyone without arousing the slightest suspicion.'

'Well, let's hear it, for crissake.'

And Fernworthy told him . . .

'Well, what do you think of it?' he asked anxiously, when he had finished.

He had no cause for anxiety; Coker's expression was all excitement and admiration.

'Man, you're a genius!'

'You really think it will work? The card trick we saw that chap doing last night gave me the inspiration.'

'Yeah, I get the point. As to will it work; well, I'd say there's a lot of imponderables in this scheme of yours, Ed. A lot of factors that will just have to be left to chance. On balance I'd say that the chances of success are better than evens.'

'And if we fail,' said Fernworthy. 'If, by sheer bad luck, we don't get the opportunity to make the snatch, we'll be completely in the clear. We just write the whole thing off to experience and walk away scot free.'

'That's right.'

They sat in silence for a while, and Fernworthy communicated with the blonde in the bar at the *Folies Bergère*, whose round, ingenuous eyes gazed out at him blankly.

Presently, Coker said: 'By the way, I have been boning up on Marx. Got this book out of the public library this morning. Ed, the factual background on that guy is really stunning. For a guy who founded the principal religion of the twentieth century, Marx fell short of perfection in many regards. Would you believe he cheated on his wife with the hired help, whom he put in the family way? To me, it's very ironic that the whole goddam world should be stood on its ear by a guy who was groping the hired help as soon as his wife went out the room.'

The crocodile of schoolgirls straggled past again, and submitted Coker's brawny form to another mass inspection.

'I shall need a fake employment card,' said Fern-worthy. 'And so will you. Is that any problem?'

'No, indeed,' said Coker. 'There's a big traffic in employment cards for aliens. Some are stolen, some forged. The best ones, the up-market ones, belonged to guys who are now dead. I can pick up a couple for around ten to fifteen pounds and we can be in business by the end of the week. But, hey, what about – you know – your hand? Won't that be a bar to you picking up a job at the cemetery?'

Fernworthy dropped his eyes, and said: 'I shouldn't think so. The wages they pay for a job like a park or cemetery keeper – which means going around picking up bits of paper and scaring off rowdy kids – is so miserable that most chaps would prefer to be on National Assistance. They'll be glad to have me – cripple though I am,' he added bitterly.

'Sorry I brought it up, Ed,' said Coker. 'But while we're on it we might as well stick with it. I'll tell you another thing you're not going to like . . .'

'What's that, Jay?'

'We need another guy to help work the plan. If any snags crop up, we're stuck with only one and a half pairs of hands and egg all over our faces.'

'I'm sure we'll be able to manage, Jay.'

'Listen, feller. For my sake – *please*!'

Fernworthy nodded. 'I suppose you're right. But how do we go about finding someone?'

'What we need,' said Coker, 'is one of those nuts who

advertises that he's willing to take on anything short of crime.'

'But this isn't short of crime. It's very *long* on crime!'

'Not in my book it ain't. And there's many who would think likewise. What we're indulging in is a little ideological redistribution. For profit.'

'Let's go and buy a paper,' said Fernworthy.

They left the National Gallery and purchased an evening paper on the corner; took it to Trafalgar Square and sat on the edge of a fountain bowl, where Fernworthy scanned the small ads.

'Here's our man,' he said at length. 'And he doesn't even specify that it mustn't be criminal.' He passed the paper to his companion.

> I am 28. Black belt in judo and karate.
> Need £20,000 immediately to buy yacht
> and sail round the world. Any project
> considered. Box No. X/2353.

'That's the guy for us, right enough,' said Coker. 'He has the high, wide smell of a nut. We'll interview him, tell him just enough to get a reaction, then decide if we can trust him – nut or no nut – with the whole deal.'

They bought a packet of envelopes. Fernworthy scribbled a message to Box No. X/2353 on a page from his notebook, and they posted it there and then.

After they had parted company, Fernworthy was seized with a compulsion to make a personal pilgrimage to the gallery just off Bond Street that had a small Boudin for sale. He had several times been to see it, for the notion that a masterpiece such as it could be bought for money exercised a curious fascination upon him.

It was still there. Quite small. A view of the beach

at Trouville, with several groups of tightly-knit figures, a couple of umbrellas and a white dog, the splash of a tricolour flag. The whole world contained within a picture frame.

There was a young woman seated at a desk. She looked up from pounding a typewriter when Fernworthy gave an exploratory cough.

'Yes?' she demanded coldly.

'The Boudin,' said Fernworthy. 'How much?'

She gave him an affronted stare, opened a drawer of the desk and took out a calf-bound ledger, which she consulted.

She smirked pityingly. 'Thirty thousand pounds,' she said.

'Thirty thousand,' repeated Fernworthy. 'That's very reasonable for an undoubted Boudin. I shall have to think about it.' And he walked out of the shop.

It would be his. After he and Jay had done their little 'ideological redistribution', there would be money in plenty to indulge his tastes in art. He paused at the kerb, as an expensive-looking sports car slid past with an attractive redhead at the wheel. Not to mention the portals of hymen, he added.

Three evenings later, he met Coker in a quiet pub off St Martin's lane that was frequented by actors and homosexuals, and seldom filled up before nine o'clock. Coker put in an appearance at six-thirty.

'No sign of our guy yet?' he asked, looking round the empty bar.

'I wrote that he was to be here at six forty-five on the dot,' said Fernworthy. 'And wearing a red carnation. It will provide a test of his punctuality. What are you going to have to drink?'

'I'll get it. Listen – how did you make out at the

cemetery with the phoney employment card?'

'No problem at all,' said Fernworthy. 'As I'd sur-
mised, they have the greatest difficulty in getting people.
I'm to do five shifts a week, nine till five. They give me
a peaked cap, and like me to wear a dark suit. All I
have to do is walk round with a pin on the end of a
stick and pick up bits of paper. That and chase away
dogs and kids. And I start Monday.'

'Great!'

Three more people come into the bar in the next ten
minutes, but none wearing a carnation. On the stroke
of the quarter hour, the street door swung open. Coker
looked out over the top of his raised glass and swallowed
some beer the wrong way.

'Omygawd! We didn't bargain for *that*!'

Box No. X/2353 was dead on time, was wearing the
requisite red carnation. And was a woman.

A young and extraordinarily pretty woman. Magnolia-
skinned and raven-haired. Possessor of large and luminous
eyes under a dramatic curve of eyebrows, richly pig-
mented. She could have passed for a Creole, but the
straight, high-bridged nose was pure Greek. She wore a
hip-hugging skirt and a striped blazer. The carnation
was in the blazer buttonhole.

She paused at the door and looked about her, scanning
the people who stood at the bar, her head – the dark
hair spanned by a bandeau after the mode of the 'twenties
– turning this way and that, her long-lashed eyes missing
nothing. They lit upon Fernworthy and Coker staring at
her in slack-mouthed dismay from the far corner.

She smiled and went over to them. She had the swaying walk of a long-legged, healthy girl.

'I can see from your expressions that I've come as
something of a shock,' she said. Her voice was deep,
cool and cultured. 'You addressed me as "dear sir" in

the letter, but I came nevertheless. May I sit down?'

'Forget it, baby,' said Coker, not unkindly. 'The job calls for a man.'

'Not necessarily,' interposed Fernworthy.

'Oh, come on, Ed!'

'We'll give her a chance,' said Fernworthy. He took out his pocket watch and laid it on the table before him. 'Young lady, you've got five minutes to sell yourself. At the end of that time, if my colleague and I are sufficiently impressed, we might – I say *might* – put our proposition to you.'

The young woman sat down facing them both, crossed her legs with unselfconscious elegance, rested her chin in a well-manicured hand. 'I lied about the judo and karate,' she said. 'That was just a come-on to attract a customer. And I need a yacht to sail round the world like I need a hole in the head.'

'Did you also lie about your age?' grinned Coker.

'No,' she said. 'Or, if I did, I'm sticking with it. But I do need the money. I desperately need the money, but I'm not saying why. So much for the content of my ad. Now, the real me: my name's Angela Carruthers and I was born in Richmond. Educated at a private school. Eight O-Levels and three A-Levels. Read English at Exeter University, got a second-class degree. Five years as an advertising copy-writer, specializing in travel agency accounts. And eighteen months in jail.' She delivered her punch line in the same calm, flat tones as she had spoken the rest.

Fernworthy and Coker exchanged raised eyebrows.

'May one be permitted to know for what you were imprisoned, dear lady?' asked Fernworthy.

'For fraud,' she replied. 'I was mixed up in a racket of selling seaside holiday villas in Spain. They only existed in the artist's impressions that were splashed all over brochures. The actual site was a mosquito-infested swamp twenty miles inland. After we'd sold the last plot, my boss upped and fled with the loot, leaving me to face the music. I'm not beefing, but I reckon the world owes me around twenty thousand pounds. If you gentlemen can put me in the way of a similar sum, you can have my not inconsiderable talents as an ideas-person at your disposal. But there's one proviso : I don't want to see the inside of that bloody prison again.'

She uncrossed her legs and folded her hands upon her lap, looking from one to the other of them amiably.

Fernworthy coughed and said : 'Miss Carruthers . . .'

'Mrs Carruthers,' she corrected him. 'My boss – the bastard – who ran off with the loot, was also my husband.'

'Mrs Carruthers, would you be so kind as to withdraw for a few moments, so that I can confer with my colleague ?'

'Certainly,' she replied, getting up. 'I'll be over by the bar when you want me.'

They watched her go.

'Nice girl,' said Coker. 'And she's got class.'

'I think,' said Fernworthy, 'that she may have something to contribute to our enterprise. Apart from being an extra pair of hands, she's a young woman with a head on her shoulders. Personally, I'm in favour of trying her with the proposition – just the way we planned it.'

'I'll go along with that,' said Coker. And he wagged his finger at the figure in the striped blazer by the bar. She came back to them.

'Well, do I get the job ?' she asked.

'You get a peek at the proposition,' said Coker.

'I will unfold it to you gradually,' said Fernworthy. 'Bringing it into sharper focus with every phrase. If the proposition interests you, you will wish to stay and hear me out to the end. If you are *not* attracted by the proposition, you will wish to get up and walk out of this bar the moment that you have heard enough to put you off. It goes without saying that, in the latter eventuality, we ask that you respect our confidences and never breathe a word of what you have heard. Is that agreeable to you?'

'Sure,' said Mrs Carruthers.

'To begin,' said Fernworthy, 'is it legal? No, it is not legal. You are still here, Mrs Carruthers.'

'Keep talking,' she said.

'Is it theft?' said Fernworthy. 'Yes, it is theft. To whom does the item in question belong? It belongs to no one, and its removal by us will cause no loss to any living person. What are we going to do with this item? We are going to put it into the hands of certain persons who will treasure it as a pearl beyond price. What is our motive for doing this? Our motive is pecuniary profit. How much profit?' He looked keenly at Angela Carruthers. The gaze of her luminous, large eyes was unwavering. 'The sum we have in mind – it is quite arbitrary – is a million pounds. Do you want to hear more, Mrs Carruthers?'

'I'm hooked,' she said. 'You'd better tell me the end of the plot.'

So they did.

They had dinner *à trois* in a cheap Soho trattoria: Spaghetti Bolognese and a large carafe of Chianti. Angela Carruthers did most of the talking: they soon discovered that she was a great talker, with a mine of ideas that tumbled from her lips half-formed; were assembled in the air and given shape by her eloquent gestures, her infectious enthusiasm.

Over coffee and brandy, she extemporized upon the question of disposing of the precious remains.

'I don't go along with offering the entire deal to the Soviets,' she said. 'To me, this breaks the primary rule of marketing, which is to maximalize the product and likewise the outlets. Jay, how many bones – individual pieces of bone – are there in the human skeleton?'

'Ah, it's not a figure I've ever worked out,' said Coker. 'But I can give you a rough idea. That's – ah – twenty-three vertebrae, twelve ribs a side, that's forty-seven for a start. Then you've got the skull and jawbone, two halves of the pelvis, three principal bones per arm, plus finger-bones. And a similar arrangement for each leg. Then you have collar bones and shoulder-blades. I have already lost count, but I'm thinking somewhere way over a hundred pieces.'

'Over a hundred items of merchandise,' said Angela Carruthers. 'And ranging in size and consumer interest from the skull, which I take to be the prime sales draw, to a humble knuckle bone.'

'You really think we should offer him piecemeal?' asked Fernworthy. 'And to whom?'

'The whole world – the whole Communist world – is our market,' she said. 'Russia and her satellites, of course. Red China and a large part of South-East Asia. Then we have Cuba. The Communist parties of the Western world. All of these parties and organizations have inexhaustible funds. No matter what part of the Marxist spectrum they occupy: Maoist, Stalinist, Trotskyist, Leninist, or what have you, they all look to the Founder for their prime inspiration. Ed, here, is quite right in his original assertion: that Marx's remains are to be compared with the most revered saintly relics of the Christian world. They will be frantically sought after. They will be fought over. The faithful will pay and pay and pay to obtain them. I can see our prospectus now. Our sales brochure, which will be circulated throughout the world. I shall write the copy, of course. I tell you, the *real* work will begin when we have obtained the merchandise, which, thanks to Ed's inspired plan, will be relatively easy – given all the luck. Advertising the goods, vending the goods, delivering the goods and picking up the cash – *that's* where our heartaches begin.'

She paused and took a sip of her coffee. The two men gazed at her covertly, and in admiration; both feeling drawn to her, not only by reason of her manifest attractiveness of face and figure, but by the triumphant forcefulness of her will and enthusiasm. To Fernworthy, it seemed a far cry from their first, fumbling attempts to put flesh and bones upon the ghost of an idea. In the slender and capable hands of Angela Carruthers, the proposed Karl Marx coup had become a smoothly-running modern marketing enterprise. Big business. He shuddered to think of the botched job he and Coker might have made of it without her to guide them.

Still, the merchandise was yet to be obtained . . .

'I was thinking,' he said, 'that we must take advantage of August Bank Holiday. Officialdom, the Establishment, the whole country, will be *en pantoufle* that week-end, and we must really use that opportunity to increase our chances.'

'I entirely agree,' said Angela Carruthers.

'Add to that,' said Fernworthy, 'we also have the extra hour's closing of the cemetery on the Sunday, and it doesn't reopen till one on Bank Holiday Monday afternoon. I propose we commence operations on the Sunday night.'

'Right on both counts,' said Angela. 'Considering what has to be done in the first stage of the operation – or, rather, what has to *appear* to have been done – the extra hour will provide that grave note of verisimilitude that distinguishes a good, round successful lie from a shame-faced fib. Yes, let's drink to August Bank Holiday.'

And so they did, raising their glasses and pledging the health of the plan, of each other – coupled with the name of the old adulterer up in Highgate Cemetery.

V

THE AUGUST BANK HOLIDAY week-end coincided with the apogee of a drought in Northern Europe that brought water riots in Paris and Brussels, and stand-pipes to the English West Country.

On Sunday at 4 p.m. precisely, Edgar Fernworthy put aside his peaked cap and his stick with a pin on the end, and was present at the ceremony of closing the cemetery, where, after checking that there were no visitors left wandering in its bosky walks, or nodded off to sleep by the graves, the last bell was rung and the gates closed and locked. Fernworthy then gave and received farewells from his cemetery colleagues and set off down Swains Lane to find somewhere that sold a cup of tea.

The hot night fell over London N6, bringing lovers out on Hampstead Heath to romance under the Milky Way; and every pub garden was ablaze with fairy lights and resounding to the chink of glassware, the bumble-bumble of mutual admiration.

At eleven forty-five, Fernworthy went again to the gates of the cemetery, which he opened with a key that he had had copied from the original – temporarily purloined from the pocket of the head keeper a week previously.

Coker arrived five minutes later, and Angela Carruthers punctually on the hour. They entered soundlessly, and Fernworthy relocked the gates against night intruders, such as tramps and courting couples, for whom a sleeping cemetery offers many advantages.

'Did you bring all the equipment?' whispered Fernworthy, as they crept silently down the grass verge of the path that led to the grave – *his* grave.

'Checked it through three times,' said Coker. 'It's all in here.' He was hefting an extremely large suitcase.

'I think we ditch the case over the wall when we've done,' said Angela. 'The last thing we want is for Jay to get stopped for a spot check by some keen young copper who wants to know why he's carrying a suitcase through Highgate in the middle of the night.'

'Good thinking, Angela,' said Fernworthy admiringly. Really, he thought, she had become a most valued member of the little team. Her articulate expertise in all matters relating to marketing, merchandising, advertising, journalism, the media generally, reduced both of them to awed silence and total acquiescence. And all done with such good-humoured and buttonholing charm, with no suggestion of 'swank' or 'side'; but almost suggesting that one had thought of all those good ideas oneself, or, if one had not, one had been just about to do so. A most admirable young woman, thought Fernworthy. And, as he glanced sidelong at her in the bright midsummer moonlight, in her black shirt and slacks, her black sneakers and black bandeau, a most appetizing creature.

They came to the humped bulk of the Marx monolith, and it seemed bigger than Fernworthy had ever seen it before. Something of his euphoria left him. What they were about to do – the preliminaries – presented no real problems; what lay ahead – the agonizing encounters with chance – loomed terrifyingly opaque.

'Well, here goes,' said Coker, lowering his heavy suitcase. 'Let's get this show on the road. And when we've finished this, I'm gonna need a drink.'

He opened the suitcase : took out a sharp, crescent-shaped instrument set upon a spade handle that is used for cutting turfs of grass, and with it a spade. The former he passed to Fernworthy, the latter to Angela Carruthers. 'Get to work, my children,' he said.

Fernworthy was well able to use the turf-cutter one-handed. It was simply a matter of slicing into the grass with a sharp tap of the foot. In no time, he had cut the rectangle of drought-dried greenery surrounding the plinth of Marx's bust into foot-wide strips. Mrs Carruthers followed after with the spade, carefully lifting away turfs at one square foot and piling them neatly in the pathway. In this manner, they quite quickly reduced the perimeter of the grave to bare earth.

'Take a rest, folks,' said Coker, spitting on his hands. 'What we need now is a reasonable pile of loose earth lying about – there.' And he pointed to the edge of the path in front of the grave.

Fernworthy found that he was sweating slightly after his efforts, for he was still wearing his dark suit that the cemetery authorities favoured. For his own task of digging away a tilth of earth and making it into a rough pile, Coker had stripped off his shirt. Underneath, his muscled torso was thickly pelted with sandy-coloured curls, like a Koala bear. Some prompting of delicacy caused Fernworthy to interpose his own body between the sight of the half-naked digger and Mrs Carruthers.

'Nervous, Angela?' he asked her.

She shrugged. 'In fact, I'm terrified,' she said. 'I'm afraid I don't have the criminal mind. Now, you should have had my lousy husband here. Right close up to wrongdoing, he positively glows with relaxation and well-being.'

She had scarcely spoken of the missing Mr Carruthers, and neither he nor Coker had raised the topic. One presumed that she was either still in love with him and missing him greatly, or that she hated his guts and was glad to be shut of him – with the eighteen-month jail sentence thrown in as a passport to freedom.

Fernworthy said : 'I'm quite sure the criminal mind, like the mind of any performing artist, is perfectly susceptible to stage fright. Indeed, I would have thought that the more considerable the artist, the greater the nervousness in the instants before the conductor's baton descends for the opening chord of the overture.' He recalled his many years of performances, culminating in the fatal appearance at San Pantaleone, Ravello. And shut his eyes in agony.

'How would you possibly know that, Edgar?' demanded Angela Carruthers blandly. But he was saved from a reply by the sound of Coker throwing down his spade.

'I reckon that will do for the loose earth. Now we fix the sling.'

He brought out from his suitcase a stout length of steel wire rope with steel-ringed eyelets spliced into each end, into each of which was fastened a heavy shackle. Holding it in both hands, he gazed up at the massive iron head critically.

'Are you having second thoughts about the method?' asked Fernworthy with a touch of anxiety.

'I'm thinking,' said Coker, 'that we should maybe have used ring bolts, let into the side of the stonework. It would have taken longer, drilling the holes and screwing in the bolts. But I have the feeling that ring bolts would have looked more – *sincere* – than merely a wire sling.'

'It's the artist in you,' declared Fernworthy approvingly.

'Slings have an immediacy that appeals to me,' said Angela Carruthers.

'Albeit, we are stuck with the sling,' said Coker, 'since it is all we have. Would you both kindly give me a leg up while I fix it in place?'

Fernworthy bent his back. Angela took Coker's ankle, and he eased himself up and mounted. Eye to eye with the begetter of *The Communist Manifesto*, he lifted the wire sling and draped it about the thick, iron neck and made a loop in the two ends, afterwards letting them fall loose.

He jumped to the ground. All three of them looked up.

'I think,' said Fernworthy, 'that a bit of discreet chipping of the stonework – nothing that will permanently disfigure the monument, I hasten to add – will heighten the effect.'

Angela said: 'May I suggest a clod of earth, rubbed lightly across the Master's beard and nose, as if from contact with the ground?'

'Yes, to both,' said Coker. And taking a hammer and chisel, he proceeded to incise several small chips in the massive base, at the corners and edges. He regarded his handiwork with head on one side critically. 'How's that?'

'A bit more off here,' suggested Fernworthy, pointing.

'Like – that?' Chip went the hammer and chisel, and a fragment flew off.

'Fine.'

'Now for the clod of earth.'

By an unspoken consent, the two men raised Mrs Carruthers aloft, and she with two handfuls of North London clay, which she smeared over the bulbous end of the iron nose and on the tip of the unkempt, fan-shaped beard. They then lowered her to the ground.

'Any more business?' said Fernworthy.

They gazed up at the great head, and it seemed to Fernworthy – and it was the lightest of fancies – that a whisp of cloud passing in front of the full moon, caused

an angry shadow to cross the unseeing eyes of the iron
mask above them.

'Any other embellishment,' said Angela Carruthers,
'would be to gild the lily and draw undue attention to
our stratagem.'

'Leave well alone,' said Coker.

'In that case,' said Fernworthy, 'I declare that the
Ace of Spades has been drawn from the pack, and that
we have indeed raised him up – as far as the world is
concerned.'

Half an hour later, the three of them sat on a low wall
in downtown Highgate, close by the underground station.
And there Coker opened a bottle of non-vintage champagne which Angela had purchased for the occasion.
'Here's to us!' said the big American. 'There's none like
us!'

They toasted each other and the onward success of
the enterprise. Then they parted, each his and her
separate ways.

On the Monday morning – it being Bank Holiday
Monday in the United Kingdom, except Scotland –
Angela Carruthers left her flat in South Kensington
and telephoned the Home Office, Whitehall. In due
course, she was passed from mouthpiece to mouthpiece,
till she eventually had the undivided attention of a duty
Assistant Secretary. The time was ten-thirty a.m.

'Hallo, yes?'

'I am speaking from a phone box near Highgate
Cemetery,' said Angela. 'Listen to me carefully. My
associates and I have stolen the remains of Karl Marx.
What was that you said?'

Although the Assistant Secretary was relatively young
and newly-promoted – and how else would it have fallen
to him to have been on duty on the Bank Holiday? –

he was not of the kind to panic and go off half-cock, which in his particular department of the Home Office was equated to making frantic telephone calls to Scotland Yard, which meant that the heavy mob from Fleet Street were never far behind; instead, he telephoned around for the Assistant Under Secretary of State who was his immediate chief, finally running him to earth in the bar of his golf club. This worthy was none too pleased to be called away from his early morning drinking, and the sound of jollification in the background was no help to understanding.

'They have stolen *what*?' he demanded.

'Sir, they claim to have stolen the remains of Karl Marx. The Communist, you know.'

'I am perfectly aware who Karl Marx was. Who have stolen him, and why?'

'The young woman claimed to be a member of an extreme right-wing organization. She says the remains will be destroyed unless HM Government pay a ransom – as yet unspecified. She said she would be in touch later.'

'What have you done about it so far, on your own initiative?'

'Why – er – nothing, sir.'

'Excellent. Continue along those lines, and most of all do not inform the Yard. I take it that the grave has not yet been inspected?'

'Er – no, sir.'

'Your prudence continues to gratify me. Have it done immediately. Send the best man you have available. And a pathologist, if you can lay hands on one today. Have them inspect the site and come up with a specific answer to the specific question: Have the remains been removed, or is it a hoax? Telephone the answer to me here. To me and no one else, do you understand? If this thing has really happened, the Home Secretary must hear it from my lips, and not from the front pages of tomorrow's gutter press. Do I make myself clear? This thing is either nothing – or it is dynamite!'

Fernworthy had let himself into the cemetery and was lurking in the bushes by the gate, his peaked cap and staff of office ready to hand. When he saw the black Rover 2000 brake sharply to a halt outside, he sauntered casually across the path, so that he was in full view of the two men who leapt out of the car and pressed their faces to the railings.

'I say, you there! Will you open up?' called one of the newcomers.

Fernworthy assumed the sly and non-co-operative air that comes with a very little authority and a peaked cap.

'Cemetery's shut,' he said gruffly, pointing to the signboard. 'Can't you read? "Sundays, Christmas Day, Good Friday, Bank Holidays: one p.m. to four p.m." Today's Bank 'oliday Monday and we ain't open till one.'

'This is the Home Office.'

'The what?'

'The Home Office. Look, man. Here's my pass. Read it, read what it says here.'

Sulkily, Fernworthy shambled up to the gate, gazed morosely at the plastic-covered card that was shoved under his nose. He read it right through. It proclaimed John Edward Sargent to be on the business of Her Majesty's Secretary of State for the Home Department, and was signed by that august gentleman – in ink. It instructed Whom It May Concern to let J. E. Sargent pass without let or hindrance, and made further demands of such a sweeping nature as to cause Fernworthy to blink. He fumbled for the key and opened the gates

without further ado. J. E. Sargent and his companion
brushed past him.

'Which way to Marx's grave?'

'Who?'

'Karl Marx, you fool!' Sargent was a man of middle
years who had been dragged from his suburban garden,
and was in no mood to treat with men in peaked caps
who pick up paper with pins on the end of sticks. 'The
grave of Karl Marx – where is it?'

'Right down at the bottom,' said Fernworthy, pointing.

'Come on, Doctor,' said Sargent, and set off at a brisk
walk. Fernworthy followed after them, quickening his
gait till he was abreast of the man from the Home Office.

'What's the fuss, mister?' he asked.

'Marx's grave – have you seen it this morning?' rasped
Sargent. 'Has it been disturbed?'

'Disturbed? Dunno. Haven't been near it,' said Fernworthy guilelessly.

'That's it up ahead,' said the doctor, pointing. 'I
recognize it from the pictures.'

They drew close. Sargent swore a four-letter word
under his breath, and Fernworthy exclaimed:

'Cor! What's that thing round his neck?'

'It's a sling, you fool!' snarled Sargent. 'And all the
ground's been dug up. Doctor, I think we've got trouble
here!' He went up to the monument and looked up at
it, and all about it. 'They've had this thing over on its
face, no doubt at all. It had to be a crane. See how the
head's smeared with mud? But how in the hell did they
get a large portable crane in here during the night?'

'It could still be a hoax,' said the doctor. He was a
Home Office pathologist, and a man trained to doubt.
'Why did they bother to replace the monument?'

'That's no help to me,' growled Sargent. 'My chief

wants a specific answer, not speculations. That thing's got to come off again, Doctor, and you've got to make a head-count – ' he narrowed his eyes to read the inscription on the plinth – 'of everybody in there.'

'You'll have to have to get on to the Council,' said Fernworthy. 'The Council crane does all the big jobs in here.' He pointed to an angel in white Carrara marble. 'They put that up last Thursday,' he added irrelevantly.

'The Council will scarcely be operating a crane service on Bank Holiday Monday,' said the pathologist mildly. He was a good-humoured man who was quite enjoying the situation.

'Oh, you'd be surprised what they do,' said Fernworthy. 'They keep a duty crane going right round the clock. In case of a bad traffic smash-up and such things, you see.'

The man from the Home Office whirled round, pointed a commanding finger at the figure in the peaked cap.

'Where's this crane to be had?' he demanded.

Fernworthy quenched a desire to smile from pure pleasure. Instead, he drew a very deep breath before replying, and fumbled in his breast pocket for a scuffed notebook.

'I've got the phone number of the yard right 'ere,' he said. 'Always keep it by me, alonger the undertakers, monumental masons and suchlike.'

Sargent had made his call from a phone box, and had been informed that, it being a Home Office matter, the crane would be sent immediately. Re-entering the gates, he found that his doings had attracted the attention of a patrolling police constable, who looked pointedly at the parked car, at the part-open gates, at the notice board. Fernworthy, who was watching from the background, swallowed hard.

'May I ask what you're about, sir?' demanded the policeman.

Sargent clicked his tongue with annoyance and produced his card. It had a salutory effect upon the policeman, who handed it back with a smart salute.

'Do you need my assistance, sir?' he asked. 'Shall I call for reinforcements?' His hand stole, longingly, towards the walkie-talkie attached to his breast.

'No reinforcements,' said Sargent. 'But I would like you to keep guard on the gates, and admit only a Council portable crane that is due here shortly.'

'Council crane, sir. Yes.'

'This is a highly confidential matter, Officer,' said Sargent. 'It comes under the Official Secrets Act. Need I say more?'

'Right you are, sir!' said the policeman, wide-eyed with awe. And to reinforce his emotions, he saluted again.

Fernworthy walked back to the grave with the man from the Home Office, and there they found the pathologist reclining on a grassy bank in his shirtsleeves, enjoying the sunshine. It was ten minutes to twelve by Fernworthy's watch. In just over an hour's time, as he knew, the head keeper would come and open up the cemetery. From that moment on, there would be too many actors in the charade.

For vastly different reasons, Sargent was thinking about the time.

'Will it take long, Doctor – this head-count?' he asked.

The pathologist squinted across at the inscriptions. 'What you have in there – or should have, considering the years that have gone past – are five perfect skeletons,' he said. 'Provided they're not too far down, and not jumbled up, it will be a matter of moments to identify the remains of the only adult male.'

Fernworthy remembered having heard that before.

'We might still be through in time for lunch,' said Sargent. 'God, I could do with a drink. This damned heat gets me down.'

There came the harsh coughing of a heavy diesel.

'Here's the crane,' said the pathologist.

Fernworthy's heart quickened its beat most disturbingly. Restless with anxiety and tension, he walked swiftly up the path to meet the oncoming crane, which was advancing towards him at a smart rate. It was painted brown and had the legend *Highgate Borough Council* and its coat of arms painted along the side of the chassis. Jay Coker was at the steering wheel, driving with grinning exhilaration. He was wearing denim overalls and a baseball cap, and winked at Fernworthy *en passant*, then slewed the big rig to a halt before the grave of Karl Marx.

'I asked for at least two men,' growled Sargent. 'There's some digging to be done here, also.'

'I took your call, boss,' responded Coker cheerfully. 'On account of there ain't nobody on duty but yours sincerely. I brought me a spade. I'm a great little digger. This the thing you want off? Yeah, I see it's already been off, the sling's still in place. I wonder who could of . . . ?'

'Don't do any wondering,' said Sargent. 'Leave the wondering to me and move that monument.'

'Okay, boss.'

He used the sling that he had himself put there: connected the looped ends to his hook and took the strain. The steel wire rope creaked taut. The crane rocked on its chassis. Nothing happened for a moment; then Fernworthy felt the small hairs at the back of his neck suddenly go stiff – as the great iron head and its stone plinth swayed a little, seemed about to topple, and then rose slowly into the air. The jib of the crane moved through an arc of about thirty degrees, and its burden was gently lowered to rest in the middle of the path.

Coker cut the engine and got down from the driver's seat, bringing a hefty spade with him.

Sargent and the pathologist were examining the flat rectangle of bare earth that had been revealed.

'This hasn't been dug out for donkey's years,' said the man from the Home Office, taking a tentative dig with the heel of his shoe.

'I wouldn't like to lay a lot of money on that, boss,' said Coker, spitting on his hands and hefting the spade. 'This clayey soil is mighty compressible and that's one helluva weight we've taken off it. Mind your backs, gentlemen. Make way for the workers!' He drove the blade into the yielding earth and lifted a large spadeful.

Fernworthy turned and walked away. Now that the hoped-for moment had come, some delicacy of feeling obtruded upon his excitement. He was, he had to admit it, squeamish about death and the appurtenances of death. Always had been. Leave it to Coker, who had been a medical student. One heard that they took their lunch break in the dissecting rooms, munching on their peanut butter sandwiches, a book propped up against a cadaver. Each to his own. Best think of that gem of a Boudin that awaited him in the gallery off Bond Street. The quiet ladies with the parasols, the sky of illimitable blueness, the splash of colour of the tricolour. A window upon a time and a place. Priceless in essence, but available to him for thirty thousand pounds.

There was a languid stillness in the air. It reminded him of the South of France. There should be cicadas chirruping in the long grass, and the slate roofs of Highgate should instantly turn into the russet pantiles of the Midi. He would go back there soon. The nights always attracted him: dinner at the Hôtel de Paris, *dorade au four à la pêcheur,* or perhaps *caneton nantais à l'orange,* a bottle of *Château Ste-Roseline.* Then a stroll across the square, with the palm trees waxen green in the lamplight, to the Casino. He had done it so often in the old days, in the days of his 'former discipline'; but then he had been a parasite upon the elegant, evening-dressed clientele of the *salons privés,* and it had been a wonder – and a tribute to his art – that he had never once aroused the suspicion of the watchful physiognomists at the entrance; but it had always been : '*Bonsoir, Monsieur Fernworthy. Bonne chance, Monsieur Fernworthy.*' Next time, he would be one of the gilded people upon whom he had formerly preyed. He would hazard a few *plaques.* Toss one to the croupier – '*Pour le personnel.*'   '*Merci, Monsieur Fernworthy.*' – then out into the mimosa-scented night for whatever adventures might offer themselves. In the new life that was about to open out before him there would be encounters, surely, that held out more promise than that ghastly experience in Florence all those years gone by. And that brought him to Angela Carruthers, surely the only attractive woman – indeed, the only woman of any quality whatsoever – with whom he had ever had any continuous and close relationship. He was beginning to assemble an erotic daydream that he had composed about himself and Angela (it was set in Monte Carlo, began with dinner at the Paris, and concluded with protracted variants on the theme of gentle seduction), when the sudden restarting of the diesel engine shook him to the awareness that he had strolled almost to the gates – he could see the policeman on guard outside – and a good half-hour had gone by. Turning on his heel, he walked quickly back in the direction from which he had come, and soon saw that Coker was standing by the monument, in conversation with the other two. The grave appeared to have been filled in again, and the spade was stuck in the hump of newly-laid earth.

Coker grinned at him as he drew close.

'Hi, feller,' he said. 'Seems we gotta keep our big mouths shut about what's happened here today. Me, they've got by the short hairs. I open my big mouth and I'll be deported.'

'It's not a joking matter,' said Sargent. 'A malicious hoax has been perpetrated, and it's to go no further.' He glanced pointedly at Fernworthy's stump. 'I don't suppose *you* want any trouble, either,' he added. What he meant was : as a cripple, *you* can't afford to get up the nose of authority.

'I'm saying nothing,' said Fernworthy.

'Well, it's been nice knowing you, boss,' said Coker, climbing up into the driver's seat of the crane. 'I'll get this thing back on top again, and no one will be any the wiser.'

Fernworthy held his breath, glancing sidelong at Sargent, as he knew Coker must be doing also . . .

The man from the Home Office consulted his watch. 'Doctor, I've got to phone Whitehall immediately,' he said. 'After that, I'll give you a lift to the station. That all right with you ?'

'Perfectly, my dear fellow,' replied the pathologist good-humouredly. 'Might even be back home in time for a late lunch with the family.' He smiled up at the big man on the crane, then at the anxious face under the peaked cap. 'Good day to you both. It's all been rather a waste of time, hasn't it ?'

As the two of them walked off together, Coker revved up the diesel encouragingly. They did not look back. When they were out of sight behind a line of trees and gravestones, he leapt down.

'Well?' cried Fernworthy.

The big American raised two fingers in the V-sign.

'Marx?' shouted Fernworthy over the thunder of the diesel.

Coker pointed to the grave and bellowed in Fernworthy's ear: 'Positively identified by the doc, and crosschecked by yours sincerely. And wouldn't you guess that I put him back on top? This is going to take all of five minutes flat.'

'What if that policeman comes wandering in to see how we're getting on?'

'He'll have to hurry!' Coker was already reaching for his spade.

'I think I'd rather . . .' Fernworthy gestured down the path, feeling absurdly weak and useless.

Coker only grinned. 'Take a walk,' he cried. 'If you meet the cop, keep him occupied a while by telling him about your amputation.'

Fernworthy gazed down into the brown whirlpool of his tankard of beer. He was no beer-drinker; it gave him dyspepsia. They were at the pub – *their* pub. Advertised for tonight's delights were Esmé von Berlin, everybody's favourite dragster, now top of the bill; Janine, stripper extraordinary; and the Great Fabian, conjuror supreme. Clearly, the composition of the cabaret ran on narrowly defined lines, but what of the Baffling Zoltan? And where was the surly but appetizing Sheila Dazzle? thought Fernworthy absently.

He said: 'By jove, we were lucky there, Jay. I think my heart nearly stopped beating a couple of times.'

'In that regards, you do yourself and your plan less than justice,' said Coker. He was sporting one of his Captain Kettle cigars and taking occasional, exuberant bites out of an individual pork pie. 'But you must remem-

ber that at no time have we been in any real hazard.
That was the inherent beauty of your plan, the built-in
fail-safe factor.'

'Well, I suppose so,' said Fernworthy. 'But we've
certainly been jolly lucky.'

'Lucky is putting it mildly,' said Coker. 'In the last
week or so, I have written a dozen scenarios in my mind.
You know what I mean? – how it could go, good or bad.
The way it worked out, now that was the best scenario
that ever came up in my mind. Perfect!'

'So lucky,' said Fernworthy, 'that I really think, Jay,
we could have done it straightforwardly, without bother-
ing with the trick with the Ace of Spades – now it's out of
the pack, but it's still in the pack. We could have
marched in there, me with my peaked cap and my stick
with a spike, you with your crane, and we could have
dug him up.'

Coker shook his head and swallowed a mouthful of
pie.

'A countless number of other factors could have
arisen,' he said. 'Indeed, one factor that arose today
would have blown the whole deal, but for the guy from
the Home Office.'

'And that was?'

'The cop,' said Coker.

Fernworthy nodded. 'You're right. Alone, we'd have
been stuck with him breathing down our necks.'

Coker said: 'No matter how tight a story we con-
cocted, that cop would have stuck with us, we not
possessing the muscle to make him stay outside and keep
guard. Man, that was the best part of all – having the
fuzz keep guard while we lifted Uncle Karl, put the
monument back on top.'

'Drink up, gents!' cried the barman. It was two-
thirty.

'I'd best get back to the Council yard,' said Coker. 'The other guys who work there think I'm nuts to have volunteered for duty on Bank Holiday Monday, double pay or no double pay. By the way, I figure to work out the week, then quit.'

'I shall stay till the end of next week,' said Fernworthy. 'Best if our departures overlap slightly – just in case anyone puts two and two together when we break the news to the horrified world.'

'It's a small point,' said Coker. 'But it is a nice point. If I may say so, Ed, it has the stamp of your impeccable style.'

'Thank you, Jay.'

Coker drained his glass and stooped to pick up the large zipper hold-all that lay at his feet. Fernworthy saw the movement and winced slightly.

'Did you have to – *break him up in pieces*?' he whispered.

Coker shook his head. 'The general knowledge of the average layman never ceases to amaze me,' he declared. 'He was already broke up. Do you not know that your skeleton is only held together by the connective tissues, which, when destroyed by benevolent corruption, leave you in bits and pieces, all nice and clean, like polished shards of ivory? The skeleton is a mighty beautiful creation. I'm telling you, man, there's many who look better skeletoned than whole.'

'Time gentlemen, please!' intoned the barman.

Amen to that, thought Fernworthy. There comes a time for all of us. Aloud, he said : 'I'll go and phone Angela. In the event, we didn't need her extra pair of hands for the snatch. But we're certainly going to be leaning on her expertise from here on.'

Adagio

I

IT WILL NOT have escaped the attention of such who are writing Ph.D. theses on The British Press in any of its ramifications that the *Daily Epicure* does not cater solely for the intelligentsia; but it is also sensitive to such broad issues as the vagaries of vicars, show-biz multi-marriages, blondes lured to fates worse than death in the Middle East, hoped-for scandals involving members of the Royal Family, any conjunction of ladies of easy virtue and Cabinet Ministers or members of the House of Lords, half-page pictures of young ladies with erectile nipples, and anything concerning the ill-treatment of cuddly animals. Eschewing the sacred slope of Fleet Street, the *Epicure*'s glass and concrete temple of the journalistic art lies at the south side of the Thames. The vast picture windows of its street-level showroom are a repository for visual displays of such engrossing items as winning Grand Prix cars still streaked with mud, oil and the blood of rivals; rowboats that have made a single-handed crossing of the Pacific; full-scale representations of suburban kitchens that have been the scene of hatchet murders; etcetera.

It was to this repository of modern enlightened communication that, almost three weeks to the day after the arcane events in Highgate Cemetery, Edgar Fernworthy made an anonymous telephone call and asked to speak with the editor. In the event, he was put through to the editor's personal assistant, a liberated Oxbridge graduette with whom the editor was cheating his third wife.

'Yes?'

'Young lady, my associates and I are giving you an exclusive. We have removed from its grave in Highgate Cemetery the skeleton of Karl Marx – I will repeat the name: Karl Marx – and we are offering the individual bones, piecemeal, to interested sections of Marxist-orientated political parties and groups throughout the world. Have you got that?'

'But . . . but . . .'

'Regrettably, the Home Office – by reason of the fact that there has been a recent hoax concerning the alleged removal of the Marx remains – refuse to take our assurances seriously. My associates and I, mindful of the public-spirited attitude of the *Epicure*, have selected you to expose this dilatory attitude on the part of the Establishment. Are you still there, young lady?'

'Yes – but, listen . . .'

'Mark this well: upon opening the grave, it will be seen that Karl Marx's remains have been removed. In addition, there will be found a red box – similar to the red leather-covered despatch boxes used by members of the Cabinet and their associates – in which is a coded message which will positively identify myself and my associates as those in possession of the Marx remains. Do you have all that?'

'Yes! I say – don't ring off . . .'

Fernworthy replaced the receiver of the public telephone box in the concourse at Piccadilly Underground. He gave a 'thumbs-up' sign to Angela Carruthers, who was standing outside the booth door in a very fetching red plastic mackintosh with a black plastic bandeau. She waved and nodded, then gave a 'thumbs-up' to Jay Coker, who was already poised to dial the number of another daily newspaper in the adjacent box. Upon receipt of her signal, he did just that.

'Hallo there, will you connect me with the editor? I've got a very hot exclusive. No, he won't know me . . .'

The purveying of erectile nipples and dubious tips about the Royal Family being a not unprofitable trade, the *Epicure* and her consoeurs are able to afford the most exclusive and expensive of legal advice. The titled senior partner of the firm of Bedford Row solicitors to whom the editor of the *Epicure* applied for guidance about the wisdom of printing the Karl Marx item without first clearing it with the Home Office (the editor's personal assistant was on his knee and murmuring her shorthand notes of the phone conversation into his disengaged ear), gave it as his opinion that, there having been no prior denial from the Home Office, the paper was under no moral or legal obligation to consider the feelings of that distinguished organization – in other words, let her rip. And, yes, the whole thing might well be a hoax indeed. *Caveat emptor*, dear boy. Buy it by all means, print it if you will. If it rebounds in your face, you will at least have had a run for your money on a dull Wednesday in September.

Next morning, the British Prime Minister, shuffling downstairs in Number 10, Downing Street in slippers and dressing-gown, picked up the early delivery of the day's papers and skimmed the headlines over a glass of milk in the kitchen. All the tabloids led with the Marx story.

HAS MARX BEEN BODY-SNATCHED?
Likely explosion in Communist world!

And, more coyly:

HAVE WE LOST KARL?
Fears for remains of Father of the Reds

'WE HAVE TAKEN MARX'S SKELETON!'
Exclusive phone call sets Whitehall a-tremble!

The *Daily Epicure*, with the abrasiveness that marks her out from all others, had gone back to the origins of the true fairy story and had nominated crooked sheriff and hawk-eyed vigilante:

KARL MARX SENSATION!
Home Office stands accused of negligence!
THE EPICURE DEMANDS:
WHERE IS KARL?

It was the implications of the latter that sent the Prime Minister's hand to the telephone, from whence orders were flashed down a chain of command that ended with an exchange between that same Assistant Secretary and his chief who had both been concerned with the earlier, supposed hoax.

'Have you seen the papers, by God?'

'Yes, sir.'

'Have you done anything?'

'No, sir.'

'Thank heaven! I should have known I could rely on you. It's another devilish hoax, of course. It will be found that the perpetrators are either young, coloured, or religious. There will have to be yet another exhumation. The PM demands it and is most upset. The US President was on the hot line. Said the President: "If Britain cannot take better care of Humanity's greatest scourge to date, why did we not despatch Marx's remains to be secured in Fort Knox years ago?" Are you still there?'

'Sir!'

'Arrange for the exhumation forthwith. Seal off Highgate Cemetery, if necessary requesting the Guards from Birdcage Walk and Windsor. No Press. No television. And the answer ...'

'Sir?'

'Not withstanding the results of your people's exhumation, the answer will be loud and clear : THE REMAINS OF KARL MARX ARE INTACT IN HIGHGATE CEMETERY! No other answer will be admissible. Understood?'

'Understood, sir!'

Fernworthy, Coker and Angela Carruthers were present in the crowds outside the locked gates of the cemetery when the second exhumation of the Marx grave was carried out by the selfsame HO official and pathologist who had performed the service on the previous occasion. This time, the Royal Army Service Corps provided the crane and the Royal Pioneer Corps a squad of diggers. Nor was the exhumation done openly; a tall canvas screen entirely shielded the grave from the sight of journalists and Press photographers, rogue television and cinema film cameramen who were occupying the commanding heights of the buildings beyond the cemetery perimeter. Countless frames of film solemnly recorded the ritual of the removal of the great headstone, its hoisting on high and its laying aside; the procession of four stalwarts of the RPC going behind the screen with their spades and shovels; the set faces of J. E. Sargent of the HO and his attendant pathologist as they followed after. And then – nothing.

The crowds grew restive. It had been stormy all night, and the heat and humidity was very intense. Passing among the multitude outside the cemetery railings, vendors of ice-cream and soft drinks were offering their wares at greatly enhanced prices and not being shunned on that account.

Jay Coker was drinking orange squash from a bottle. Both he and Fernworthy had stripped to shirtsleeves. Angela Carruthers looked as cool and composed as always she did. In all this crowd, thought Fernworthy, she looks the most divinely svelte. The contemplation of his female collaborator eased the nagging worry in his mind, but it had to come out in the end.

He said: 'What if the Home Office people decide, after all, to squash the whole thing? What if they deny that the remains have been taken?'

'It would profit them greatly to do so,' said Coker. 'Hell, what government wants to open a can of worms like we've handed them? Ed's right. It could be they'll do a snow job.'

'Stop worrying,' said Angela Carruthers. 'We've done all we can. Double-crossed every newspaper in London by handing them a supposed exclusive, already accused the Establishment of covering up the theft. Too many people are too hot under the collar to keep it quiet. It's bound to come out.'

'I hope you're right,' said Fernworthy. 'If this fails today, we'll never be able to get that grave opened up again.'

It was at this juncture that the observing eyes on the high buildings picked out the small procession of Pioneers emerging from behind the canvas screen, to throw aside their spades and fall upon cans of beer that had been provided. It was clear to all that, even at this moment, the vital examination of remains was being carried out.

Was Marx there, or was Marx not there? – the question was spoken into a score of microphones, and scribbled in shorthand upon innumerable notebooks.

Alone behind the screen, Sargent and the doctor had arrived at a certain conclusion. They were conferring, and with some heat and excitement. So engrossed were they, indeed, that the rapid approach of a low flying helicopter went all unnoticed by them. The flying machine, which was painted black and yellow, and emblazoned down both sides of its fuselage with the logo *Daily Epicure*, contained that paper's ace photographer, who, hanging out of the open door in a jump suit and crash helmet, camera in hand, pressed the shutter upon the tight scene inside the enclosing screen of canvas. The resultant picture, when rushed through the developer back at the glass and concrete monstrosity south of the river twenty minutes later, showed the two mummers in the soundless mime by the open grave. Both were staring, wide-eyed, up into the camera lens. And in the hand of J. E. Sargent was a leather-covered despatch box such as government departments use. Taken with colour film, its startling redness stood out against the dun-coloured, tumbled earth.

The *Epicure* ran a special evening edition. It was on the streets by the time Edgar Fernworthy and his two associates were back in the West End. The picture filled the entire front page, and the tell-tale despatch box was ringed and arrowed.

THE PROOF! screamed the headline.
And : HE'S GONE ! !

'We've taken the lead in this thing,' said the *Epicure*'s editor-in-chief, 'and we're going to keep it.'

The editor-in-chief had flown in from his holiday in Marbella that morning. Forty years from being a whizz kid, he knew every means to entice pennies from the customers, and what he did not know he dredged up by instinct.

'Do we offer a reward for its return?' asked someone.

'We need a slogan.'

'Requiem for a dead Hun?'

'Another literary allusion like that will get you back on the comic-strip page.'

The editor-in-chief looked round the ring of faces. Not an idea in sight. He extemporized. 'A reward's out,' he said. 'The *Epicure* is not in business to take a political stance on this thing. If and when the kidnappers are caught, we'll outbid everyone else for an exclusive on how they did the job. I think we make the public aware of the tremendous stature of Marx in the modern world, and point up the paradox of his remains being left to moulder, unguarded, in a North London cemetery. We might imply that a thing like this could bring us close to a shooting war with the Warsaw Pact countries. Oh, and I want a Marx display in the downstairs windows. Have it done overnight. A life-sized cut-out blow-up of the man himself. And a skeleton standing alongside for comparison. Get one from a medical school. If necessary, kill somebody and take his bones. So you've already got a display on care for unmarried mothers? Throw it out. We're in business to sell the *Epicure*; those damned silly girls should have been more careful. Any more ideas?'

That night, the Presidium of the Supreme Soviet was rapidly circularized for its opinions by the chairman. The fifteen deputy chairmen, secretary and sixteen members were all of the opinion that the news from London might well be a ploy on the part of the Western Alliance to cloud the issue at the forthcoming Deep-sea Fishing Conference. It was unanimously decided to keep the news of the alleged kidnapping from the Soviet peoples.

That night, also, an eminent divine in an interview on British television, expressed the view that, taken all in all, the eventual interment of Karl Marx's remains in his spiritual home behind the Iron Curtain might be interpreted as a Christian duty, though he himself held no brief for the kidnappers. At about this time, Scotland Yard, working round the clock, had elicited the fact that a recent employee of the cemetery, one Henry Arthur Tomlinson, and a former crane driver for Highgate Urban District Council named Sydney Clark, both of whom had been present at an earlier exhumation now admitted by the Home Office, were supposed to have died in 1973 and 1975 respectively.

'The merchandise having been successfully secured,' said Angela Carruthers, 'it now remains to be vended. And I take that to be my department.'

'Hear, hear,' murmured Fernworthy.

She really did look most appetizing this morning, he told himself, in that print dress with the scooped-out neckline and sleek black hair imprisoned in a white bandeau. They were having a 'working lunch' in a cafeteria in Piccadilly. He and Coker had just come from the Office of Health and Social Security, where the big American had again been accompanied by the fecund Mrs Ducane, at the end of which encounter she had handed him five pounds and gone on her way with her offspring, born and unborn. Not for the first time Fernworthy puzzled himself as to the exact nature of the relationship between Mrs Ducane and Coker. Were they lovers? Was Coker actually living upon her drawings from Social Security? If so, then he was certainly a sponger of the very worst sort. It was all very odd. Fernworthy would have bitten off his tongue rather than

question his accomplice, and Coker appeared to find
no need to enlighten him, save to mention, on an earlier
occasion, shortly before the first, faked attempt upon the
grave, that he 'sure as hell wasn't bringing Eunice and her
big mouth into the secret'.

Angela said : 'I have sketched out the copy for the
prospectus, and I'll show you the finished piece tomorrow. I propose we send it – in the form of an advertise-
ment – to the *Epicure* and the rest of the dailies. They
will print it for free, of course, and be grateful for the
opportunity. As we've seen from the media this morning,
the great British public has taken the story to its heart.
It's the biggest thing since that gorilla gave birth at the
zoo. Not only Britain, but our friends and allies across
the Atlantic are also running the story as a lead item,
and we can rely upon a most providential acrimony that
has sprung up between our two governments to keep the
pot on the boil. Less predictable has been the attitude of
Marxists the world over, who appear to have greeted
our little coup with stunned silence. In my view, this will
rapidly change to a desperate scramble to secure the
safe return of the remains. So we keep them on the hook
for a few days – then we release our prospectus. Any
further business?'

'That about wraps it up,' said Fernworthy.

Coker drained his coffee cup. 'I've got a little private
business to attend to,' he said. 'See you here at the same
time tomorrow, folks. So long.'

Covertly, Fernworthy watched Angela's dark-lashed
eyes as they followed the progress of the big American
down the cafeteria and out of the door. It was at times
like these – the few occasions when he was briefly alone
with her – that he was most conscious of both his mutila-
tion and the disparity between their ages. And of the

fact that Coker was both whole and young. And, presumably, attractive to women, as he supposed all large and powerful males were attractive to women. Was Angela attracted to Coker? The question prompted an imp of treachery to awaken in his mind . . .

'I was a little worried about Jay at first,' he said casually. 'That woman he lives with. She seemed to me to constitute a considerable security risk.'

'Yes?' The large and luminous eyes were upon him. The perfect face was quite expressionless. No telling what was going on behind that fine brow.

'He doesn't speak about her,' continued Fernworthy. 'But one assumes that she's his common-law wife, for all that she doesn't use his name.'

'They often don't,' said Angela.

Being determined to press harder with his betrayal, Fernworthy went on: 'And she's pregnant, you see, and it occurred to me that women are often somewhat highly-strung during pregnancy, which would make her an even worse security risk. And, of course, having several rather disorderly children already, she'll have plenty to get highly-strung and hysterical about.'

'Indeed she would,' commented Angela.

'But, in the event, he's had the good sense to keep her right out of it,' said Fernworthy.

'Very sensible of him,' she said.

'I suppose, when he's picked up his share of the fortune, he'll make an honest woman of her,' said Fernworthy. And then, for good measure, putting the boot well in: 'Unless she's already married.'

'And he also, of course,' said Angela.

'That's also a possibility,' said Fernworthy. And that, he thought, just about wraps up Jay Coker's chances with this lovely creature sitting opposite.

'Well, can't sit here gossiping all day,' said Angela, picking up her handbag and treating him to her brilliant, wide-mouthed smile that would have sold a million tooth-brushes. 'You have my number, Ed. Ring me if any-thing crops up, and I'll see you here tomorrow with Jay. This time next week, we should be well on our way to our million. 'Bye for now.' She reached across and squeezed his hand. Smiled again. Was gone.

He watched the oscillations of her neat rump as she walked out of the cafeteria, and the way she placed each neat foot directly in front of the other, like a mannequin parading on a rostrum; erect, glidingly graceful.

He sighed. She was not for him, and more was the pity. One consolation – and a dog-in-the-manger con-solation it was, too – she was not for Coker either. He got up and walked out into the blinding sunlight of Pic-cadilly, where the noonday posters screamed: MARX LATEST – US DENOUNCES BRITISH SECURITY.

Attracted by the flickering of a TV screen, Fernworthy went into a bar, where he ordered a gin-and-mixed, and watched a confrontation between a news commentator and an academic who purported to be an expert on life and thought at the other side of the Iron Curtain. In response to a question, the latter gave it as his view that, given a modicum of luck, the kidnappers could scarcely go wrong, for world Marxism would pay any sum, accept any condition, for the safe return of their idol's remains. It was a declaration that should greatly have raised Fernworthy's spirits, but unaccountably it did the reverse. He downed his drink and ordered another – a large one. Never was the depressant effect of gin more clearly demonstrated, for, by his third drink, he was quite suicidal. The alcohol, however, stimulated that activity of the brain which discovers motives for be-haviour. He realized why he was miserable: it was because he was wanting Angela Carruthers. And he could not have her. Or could he?

Fernworthy bought a cinema ticket and slept the afternoon and early evening through in the centre stalls, waking only when his bladder demanded it. It was twilight when he got out, and stiflingly hot. The neon galaxy of Piccadilly was outshone by the early stars, and sparrows were chorusing in the eaves and high window-sills. Fernworthy turned into the selfsame bar that had witnessed his midday debauch, passing the newsstand and the poster that now read: MARX CRISIS – *Prime Minister Addresses Nation on TV.*

After only one drink, he knew that his resolve had not altered. Drunk or sober – and he was sober enough – he wanted Angela Carruthers and was determined to risk all by coming out in the open and making his feelings known to her. Now. This very night. He knew her address, though he had never visited her flat. It was – he glanced at the clock over the bar – a quarter to ten. One more drink, and he'd take the underground to South Kensington and knock upon her door.

How does one go about barefaced seduction? He searched the repository of his reading, of the films and plays he had seen that dealt with the question. Audacity seemed to be the order of the day in these matters. Faint heart never won fair lady – a key phrase, that. If he had persisted with that prostitute in Florence, instead of panicking the instant she undid a suspender and fleeing from her with the hastily-assembled excuse – expressed in his execrable Italian – that she reminded him too much of his mother – if he had stayed, he might well have commenced a pattern of behaviour that, by now, would have brought him to the position of an experienced seducer, instead of – it had to be faced –

that of a timid rabbit. He ordered another drink.

The man sitting next to Fernworthy on the westbound underground train was reading an evening paper whose headlines announced that the British Prime Minister, in a TV address to the nation, had stated that Her Majesty's Government held itself in no way responsible for the safe custody of the remains of a man who, notwithstanding his stature as a political thinker, had been a private citizen, nay, a person who had died within these shores, intestate and stateless. Nor would Her Majesty's Government treat with the kidnappers by expending the People's hard-earned taxes to recover Marx's remains for the nation. Let those who embrace the doctrines of Marx, the Premier had declared, stump up for the return of Marx. It must have been an impressive performance. The reminder of the enterprise upon which they were engaged served further to provide Fernworthy with an insight to his mood of depression : as soon as the money was paid over and the remains disposed of, he supposed that he would never see Angela again. Ergo, he wished the business to be protracted indefinitely. It was with this thought that he debouched from South Kensington tube station and turned his footsteps towards the maze of short streets that lie between it and Brompton Road.

He found her address quite easily : she occupied the ground floor of a quite handsome semi-detached villa, and there was her card set in a holder by the front door bell to prove it : *Mrs Angela Carruthers*. The very sight of the name had the power to stir his loins.

Fernworthy raised his finger to press the bell, then decided to take a turn round the block and give it some more thought. There was a pub round the next corner, and its beckoning lights prompted him to enter and take another drink, a large one. Leaving the pub, he continued his circumnavigation of the block, and came outside Angela's again to find that she had put on the light of the room facing the street. Her bedroom perhaps. The blind was drawn.

Another soul-searching moment poised at the bell-push was resolved in the same manner as before : one simply had to mull the thing over, get a right slant on the perspective, weigh one consideration against another. The pub was still open, and the barman expressed no surprise at the return of the wanderer, but poured him another double and opined that it must surely rain before morning.

Heavy-footed, Fernworthy completed the penultimate corner of the block. By this time, he had come face to face with the fact of his own cowardice : his proximity to the abode of his desired was no more than a callow creature's instinct to gaze through the safe barrier of a keyhole at a scene upon which he would never find the courage to open the door. He was an emotional *voyeur*, and would never, never be able to press that bell.

Rounding the last corner, he saw that he was following a tall figure who had entered the street just before him. The quite considerable amount of drink he had assimilated had both hazed his vision and slowed his reactions. It was not till the man in front paused before Angela Carruthers's door and took out a latchkey that he recognized him as Jay Coker!

It was swiftly done, with what seemed an air of total familiarity. The key in the latch, the opening and closing of the door. Dry-mouthed, Fernworthy remained rooted in his tracks, seeing their encounter flashed upon the retina of his horrified imagination : she would undoubtedly be in night attire, and it would be both insubstantial and semi-transparent; they would kiss; with odious proprietorialness, Coker would give a playful slap to her taut rump; she would squeal, and then laugh.

UNFAIR   TO   FORTY - NINE - YEAR - OLD AMPUTEES!

Tears streaming unchecked, Fernworthy took his place at the head of a marching cohort of the old, the unattractive, the shy and inhibited, the dirty-mackintoshed non-starters, the all-time losers, the smelly. 'WHY AREN'T WE GETTING IT, TOO?' their banners screamed.

The light went out behind the blind.

Fernworthy gave a sob of despair. Almost immediately after, as if the gods mocked his state, there came a flash of lightning and an immediate crash of thunder from the black overcast above. It was followed by a sudden, drenching downpour of rain.

Fernworthy ran all the way to the underground station and got soaked on the way.

II

THE FOLLOWING day's meeting of the three conspirators was overshadowed by the news – it was blazoned all over the media – that Red China had denounced the so-called kidnapping of Marx's remains as a trick on the part of the American imperialist running dogs of decadent Britain to obtain further credits from the International Monetary Fund and bolster their slave economy; though how the hard-nosed accountants of the IMF were to be influenced, one way or another, by the bones of the long-dead Father of Communism was not made clear. The remains of Karl Marx, declared Peking, had not been removed from Highgate; or, alternatively, it was a capitalist lie that Marx had ever been buried in Highgate in the first place.

'We're off to a fine start,' said Coker gloomily. He had not shaved that day and his eyes looked bleary – as Fernworthy noticed with a stab of envy and resentment. 'First the Soviets clamp down on the news and now the Chinese say it never happened. From where I'm standing, it seems like we've just rung up "no sale" to our two biggest customers.'

'It's early days yet,' said Angela. Wistfully, Fernworthy observed that she was as bright and fresh as ever, in contrast to the debauched looks of her partner of the previous night. 'Both great powers are assuming a defensive stance. Wait till they hear our proposition, wait till they are in competition with each other for possession and bidding one against the other. You'll see some change of attitude then.'

She then produced the prospectus, handing it first to

Fernworthy. It was neatly typed upon one side of a single sheet of good bond paper. He read it through, and passed it to Coker with a grunt of approval.

'I like it,' he said. 'It has a ring.'

'It's a familiar ring,' said Angela. 'I used to write copy for prospectuses that extolled the glory of misinformed encyclopaedias, pinchbeck coin collections commemorating non-events, and suchlike merchandise. First, one implies a reluctance on the part of the vendor to sell to anyone who isn't perfect in every way — like the reader. Second, while implying that the would-be purchaser is making a nice big, fat, crude investment that will practically keep him in his old age, one concedes that a swell guy like him is only in it for the spiritual values. It's a trick I learned from my unlamented husband, damn him.'

Coker lowered the prospectus.

'It can't fail,' he declared. 'I vote that we adopt this prospectus.'

'I second that,' said Fernworthy.

Angela's copy appeared in all the dailies the following morning.

A unique offer to The Committed Left

THE
MARX RELICS

A Strictly Limited Issue
Comprising the Authenticated Items
of the Ossature of
Karl Heinrich Marx
(1818 – 1883)

From time immemorial the RELIGIOUS, the DEVOUT, the COMMITTED have treasured the relics of their GODS, their LEADERS, their MASTERS. In this UNIQUE OFFER, The Workers of the World are invited bid for Authenticated Items from the Ossature (skeleton) of the most important figure in the history of Socialist Thinking, Author of *Poverty of Philosophy*, *The Communist Manifesto*, *Das Kapital*, etc. To ensure that the items reach only those who revere the name of MARX and testify to his unique importance in the annals of Socialist Thinking, the Advertisers are extending this offer only to fully paid-up members of genuine MARXIST organizations. No others need apply.

And, in deference to the high regard in which MARX is held among the Workers of the World, the Advertisers further require that the Items be Kept or Displayed in Surroundings of suitable Proletarian Good Taste. For the Committed Collector, few acquisitions could be more *permanently rewarding* than one of these Osseous Items. For, unlike other values, the values of REVERED RELICS are undiminished – indeed, they are enhanced – by the passing of time. Nevertheless, it is not first for its intrinsic value or limited rarity that the Committed Collector will wish to own one of these Osseous Items, but rather for the pleasure of possessing a RELIC OF THE GREATEST SOCIALIST THINKER EVER.

Bids for the AUTHENTICATED ITEMS OF THE MARX OSSATURE should be made through the small ads columns of the DAILY EPICURE, commencing Thursday next, the 21st September. Advertisers should state (a) Their MARXIST committal (b) The Item of the Ossature for which they are bidding, and (c) The amount IN UNITED STATES DOLLARS (no other currency will be accepted) of their offer.

ITEMS OF THE OSSATURE WILL GO TO THE HIGHEST BIDS

Within twenty-four hours, the prospectus was the talking point of the world, from London to the Outer Hebrides, from Tooting to Texas, wherever news is freely disseminated; and in those places where it is not, it became a prime item on agendas in party headquarters, politbureaux, secret conclaves.

'MARX UP FOR GRABS!' – said a New York headline. And that just about summed up the world's reactions.

On Thursday the 21st, Fernworthy had his alarm clock set to wake him at seven, which was the time when his morning newspaper fell on the mat. He spent a restless night. Waking and sleeping, his mind projected shifting images of Angela and Coker in attitudes of dalliance; the beach at Trouville; the interior of San Pantaleone, Ravello and the Liquefaction of the Blood; the stripper at the pub; poor Arthur Ealing in the wreckage of his light aeroplane. In fact, he was awake and drinking weak tea in the kitchenette of his flat when the alarm went off in the bedroom and nearly frightened him out of his skin. A minute later, the *Daily Epicure* came in through the letterbox. He snatched it up and turned to the small ads, where, under *Personal*, he began to read with ever-growing wonder and delight :

The Peasants' Collective of the village of Yang in the province of Fuchien pledge fifty per cent of next year's rice yield (estimated at value of $1000) for one finger bone. (Box No. C.1287)

$5000 is bid by the Marxist workers at the State Nitrate Processing Factory in Cienfuegos, Cuba, for a vertebra (lumbar preferred). (Box No. C.33)

The Independent Revolutionary Party of Italy (Marxist-Leninist) bid $20,000 for the skull. (Box No. I.654)

A Private Collector (C.P.) offers the sum of $500,000 for the skull, with jawbone. (Box No. T.321)

Five Thousand Chinese Peasants offer $2.00 each for possession of one rib. (Box No. M.564)

The Skull – $200,000 offered by the Marx For Peace Society of Great Britain. (Box No. B.144)

Private Collector in France (Marxist) will cap any offer made for a finger bone . . .

The Marx ads went on for three pages of ten columns each and spilled over to a fourth. Fernworthy attempted to make a count of them, but lost track somewhere in the fifteen hundreds. He decided that there could not have been less than two and a half thousand offers, and they ranged in amounts from one dollar (from a peasant woman in Honan) to a bid of three-quarters of a million (from a fringe Marxist Party in Latin America).

He washed and shaved with trembling hands, and had some difficulty in finding a piece of sticking plaster to staunch the flow of blood. Later, dressed, he ran all the way to the phone box on the corner to telephone Angela and hear her reaction to the tremendous news.

He dialled, glancing at his reflection in the mirror above the instrument. He looked pale, and a trickle of blood ran from under the sticking plaster and bedewed his collar.

'Hallo?' Her cool voice at the other end.

'Angela – ' his voice came out falsetto, so he tried again – 'Angela, it's Edgar Fernworthy. You've read the tremendous response, of course. They're bidding thousands and thousands. Angela, there must be at least two million dollars on the table. I say – are you still there?'

There was a long – or so it seemed – silence. Her voice, when it returned, was flat and strained, as if she had been struck with a sudden, dull pain.

'Yes, I'm still here, Ed.'

'Well, don't you think it's wonderful?' he cried.

'Yes, Ed. It's wonderful. Truly wonderful.' she sounded as if she might be crying.

He was about to ask her what was the matter when he had the distinct impression that she had covered the mouthpiece of the telephone in order that he should not overhear her addressing someone. Instantly he thought of Coker, and he experienced a spasm of jealous anger that was almost physical.

'Angela, do you hear me?' he cried.

'Ed, listen to me,' she replied. 'I want you to get over here right away. Something – something's come up that you must know about. Can you hear me?'

(She's decided to divorce her husband and marry that swine Coker!)

'Yes, I hear you,' he replied sulkily.

'And get hold of Jay, will you? Bring him along too.'

(Coker *wasn't* with her then!)

'Yes, all right,' he faltered. 'Er – Angela, can't you tell me what's the matter . . .?'

The phone went dead. Frantically, he dialled the number again; heard the ringing tone go out into unregarding ears. He put down the receiver and went out to find a bus to take him to Coker's place. Like himself, the big American did not possess the amenity of the telephone.

He arrived in Kilburn High Road, and a cheerful inebriate with a thick Irish accent directed him to Durward Gardens. Having disentangled himself from this misdirection with the assistance of a group of urchins playing marbles in the gutter, he came at length to a road of tall, terraced houses that ended in a blank wall topped with broken glass and the gusting chimneys of a factory beyond. Number three had an open door and a narrow hall in which were crammed empty perambulators. The uncarpeted stairs that rose straight up from the hall revealed further evidence of the heavy incidence of child-rearing that went in on number three, Durward Gardens : the stairs and landings were criss-crossed by lines of infants' nappies hanging out to dry; and as he mounted, the high, keening wail of a child rose above the blare of a radio, and was cut off in a slap and a howl of pain.

A door on the second floor had an envelope neatly taped to the door, and the name written in what he knew to be Coker's careful, backward-sloping hand : *Mrs Ducane.* He knocked on the door, and waited.

A second, louder knock brought a cry from beyond : 'Who's there?'

'Edgar Fernworthy,' he called back. A little, severe-looking woman in black passed him on her way up the stairs and gave him a suspicious glance. 'A friend of your – a friend of Jay's,' he added.

Mrs Ducane's condition had greatly advanced, and her blonde hair showed a great deal of shadow at the roots. One of her offspring clung to her hip and was being dusted with falling ash from the cigarette that dangled from her carmine lips. Another peered at Fernworthy from under the hem of her caftan. She smiled at her visitor quite amiably.

'Come on in. Jay won't be long. He's gone to the laundrette.'

'Thank you,' said Fernworthy. 'Er – what a charming child.'

He reached out to pat the head of the offspring she was carrying, because he understood this to be the done thing, but immediately withdrew his hand when the infant made to bite it.

'Place is a bloody mess,' said Mrs Ducane cheerfully. 'I had this water bed. Lovely it was for flopping about on. You know. The damn cat clawed a hole in it. Laugh! The folks in the flat below had to leave. Washed away they were.' She went into a chorus of mirth and had to cling to the chimney-piece when a paroxysm of bronchial catarrh all but choked her. There was a Siamese cat seated on top of a pile of dirty linen that overflowed a chair. It gazed at Fernworthy, crossed blue eyes narrowed in contempt.

'Happiness will be the death of me,' said Mrs Ducane hoarsely when she had recovered her breath. 'Sit down, Mr – er. Have a ciggie?'

'No, thanks. Don't smoke.'

'Sit you down then. Gerroff, Fang!' She swept the Siamese from the chair. Fernworthy gingerly lowered himself on to the pile of dirty linen and hoped for the best.

He took stock of the room, which inclined to the exotic in its décor. There was a Chinese glass bell revolving in the faint airs from the part-open window; its faint tinkle made a pleasing background to the wailing child on the floor below. The walls were painted a dark green and stuck all over with poster-sized reproductions of Dali, Mucha, Beardsley, and assorted psychedelia. There was a Tibetan prayer wheel hanging in the centre of the ceiling. A discoloured tide mark ran around the walls at ankle height – presumably a relic of the burst water-bed.

There came the sound of a lavatory being flushed, and, to Fernworthy's surprise, a youngish man in an electric blue suit and a hand-painted tie came into the room zipping up his fly. He nodded affably to Fernworthy.

'That was very nice, Eunice love,' he said. 'I'll be around for a bit more of that next month. If you're still here, that is.'

'I'll still be here,' said Mrs Ducane, looking down at her front. 'This one's in no hurry. How much do I still owe you?'

The young man took a cash book from the breast pocket of his electric blue jacket and consulted it.

'There's five-fifty still outstanding on the fridge, and another three on the transistor,' he said. 'You've cleared the hair dryer.'

'Christ, all that still to pay!' cried Mrs Ducane.

'You shouldn't have such extravagant tastes, love,' replied the other, with a wink for Fernworthy. 'Not that I'm complaining. S'long, all.' He was gone.

'That's the tally-man,' said Mrs Ducane. 'And he's got a mind like an open sewer.'

Fernworthy murmured some kind of acknowledgement of this observation, meanwhile trying to come to terms with the – to him quite unbelievable – implications of the tally-man's manner and bearing in Mrs Ducane's – and Coker's – home. He was pondering upon this when a sensation of warmth in his lower limb caused him to glance and see that one of Mrs Ducane's mobile offspring was gravely urinating against his trouser leg.

'Will you leave that gentleman alone, Floyd?' screeched Mrs Ducane, cutting short the child's ministrations with a clout across the head. At that moment, Coker walked in.

'Ed!' he cried. 'Nice to see you, feller. Did Eunice give you a cup of coffee?'

Above the screams of the child Floyd, she said: 'It never crossed my mind, what with one thing and another. What must you think of me, Mr – er?'

'It's quite all right, Mrs Ducane,' said Fernworthy. 'I've only just had breakfast. I came round in a hurry to see Jay on – business.' He fixed the big American with a conspiratorial look. 'We've got to go out,' he added. 'To South Kensington. Urgent.'

'I get you,' said Coker. 'Eunice honey, I dunno when I'll be back, but take care of yourself, huh?' He kissed her on the cheek and tousled the head of the nearest child, who clung affectionately to his leg.

'I want some money,' said Mrs Ducane. 'Give me some money, Jay.'

'Now, baby, you don't need no money,' replied Coker. 'You got all you need right here. What for do you want money, huh?'

'Jay – please!' she wheedled.

'No way, baby. No way!' He patted her gently on the rump and turned to the door. 'Let's go, Ed.'

Following after, down the stairs, Fernworthy gagged at the stench of wet washing and boiled cabbage, and thought : What kind of monster is this fellow, and what sort of *ménage* is he running up there?

On reaching the street, Coker said : 'What gives with Angela? You saw the *Epicure*? We're in. We made it – right?'

'I would say so,' agreed Fernworthy. 'Only . . .

And he told Coker of his disquieting telephone conversation with Angela. His companion did not seem overly perturbed, and Fernworthy felt that it was because he had not expressed his fears with sufficient force and clarity. 'Don't you see?' he insisted. 'She had someone with her. I'm *sure* she had someone with her!'

'Someone – like who?' countered the other.

It came to Fernworthy for the first time, and he immediately expressed it, in horror :

'Perhaps – *the KGB!*'

'Jesus! Ed, you don't think the Soviets have got on to us already?' cried Coker.

'Why not?' said Fernworthy. 'Their people are everywhere, aren't they? And, let's face it, we've not taken any great pains to cover our tracks. The more I think back to it, the more I'm sure that Angela was upset – dreadfully upset – when I spoke to her.' He stopped dead in his tracks and clutched at his companion's arm. 'Jay, you don't suppose that – that they'd been *torturing* her, do you? To find the whereabouts of you-know-what.'

The remains of the author of *The Communist Manifesto*, still in the zipper hold-all, had rested in a left luggage locker at King's Cross Station since the afternoon of the disinterment.

Jay Coker's face mirrored his own horror.

'Jeeze, Ed, don't even *think* such things!' breathed the American. 'I'm telling you that the very *idea* of torture turns me right off. Man, I'm here to inform you that the first touch of a hostile hand on my nuts, and I'm gonna sing like a canary!'

'It – it may not come to that,' said Fernworthy.

'Hark at the man!' cried Coker. 'You're darned right it won't come to that. I want out as of thirty seconds ago. As of thirty seconds ago, you lost yourself a partner!'

'You can't do that!' exclaimed Fernworthy, appalled. 'You can't back out and leave that girl – that lovely young person – to face those brutes alone. Because I daren't go into that flat of hers by myself. I'm too much of a coward.'

The big American nodded and looked deflated. 'You're right, Ed,' he said. 'We can't desert her now. Not after what we've been through together. We'll go along there with our hands wide open. Give those KGB guys the key of the left luggage locker and throw ourselves on their mercy. Hell, we might even come out of it with an Order of Lenin or something. It's for sure that those guys won't be handing Marx back to Highgate Cemetery, but will put him on the next jet to Moscow.'

'Perhaps so,' said Fernworthy doubtfully.

With the question mark still hanging over them, they journeyed by underground train to South Kensington, speaking little, and not at all about the headlines that screamed from the newspaper front pages all about them:

RUSSIA SILENT ON MARX KIDNAP
NATO Forces on the alert

Arriving at their destination, they walked slowly to the quiet road where Angela lived. It was just on opening time, and Fernworthy was prompted to suggest that they went for a drink: Dutch courage before the whistle blew and they went 'over the top'. His companion nodded agreement. They entered the pub and silently downed a large scotch apiece. Then another.

Fortified somewhat, they solemnly shook hands.

'It's a far, far better thing,' said Fernworthy.

'Give my hair to Mother,' grinned Coker, who seemed to have quite recovered his spirits. 'Geronimo! Let's go!'

The ring of the doorbell brought Angela immediately. It was obvious that she had been crying: her marvellous eyes were red and swollen and her nose was pink. To Fernworthy's surprise, she was still in night attire: a chocolate-coloured negligée with something whispy underneath in the same colour.

'Come in,' she said unsmilingly.

They followed her across a narrow hallway into a room at the rear of the house. A bedroom. Reclining in a large double bed was a dark-haired man of about thirty-five. He was seemingly naked, sported a Ronald Coleman

moustache and a dentifrice grin. His was a face of the
sort that Fernworthy's father – a man of stern Victorian-
style upbringing – had always described as having 'cad
written all over it'.

'Well, well, well,' drawled the man in the bed. 'Enter
second and third bandits. 'Morning, chaps. How's
crime?'

'Meet – my husband!' said Angela Carruthers
savagely.

Carruthers ('Call me Freddie, chaps!') had put his foot
in the door the previous evening, summoned by nothing
less than the text of Angela's prospectus.

'As soon as I clapped eyes on it, I saw the hand of
the Master,' he drawled. Angela shook him off as he
reached out and pawed at her half-bared shoulder. 'Or,
rather, the hand of the Master revealed through the hand
of the Mistress-Pupil. I taught this little gel all she
knows about the advertising game. Every phrase, every
nuance, in that prospectus comes straight out of the
brain of Freddie Carruthers. So I said to myself:
"Freddie, old son, your little wifie has come up with the
sweetest tickle since that chappie lifted the Crown Jewels
from the Tower of London." She denied it, of course,
but – ' he grinned – 'which of you two laddies is Ed?'

'I am,' said Fernworthy.

'He was listening at my side when you phoned,' said
Angela flatly. 'After that, he knew for sure.'

'Angela, I'm sorry,' said Fernworthy.

'It's not your fault, Ed,' she replied. 'It's just that –
now we're stuck with the bastard!' And she ran out of
the room.

'Poor sweetie,' grinned Freddie Carruthers. 'She's
overwrought and tired. 'Fraid I somewhat overdid the
husbandly ministration last night. Chuck over my pants,

there's a good fellow. Can't lie abed all day, not with all that lovely lolly just waiting to be picked up.'

Fernworthy found his voice. 'You are making rather a large assumption, my friend,' he said.

'Am I now, laddie?' responded Freddie Carruthers. 'Am I now?' He climbed out of the bed, revealing a long, tanned torso that fairly rippled with smooth muscle. Tiger-like.

'There's nothing in this set-up for you,' said Fernworthy. 'Right, Jay?'

'Right, Ed!' echoed Coker, folding his massive arms and measuring Carruthers with his eye.

The object of their attention slipped into trousers of Glenurquart tweed and a candy-striped shirt that was monogrammed on the breast pocket. He took up a necktie that bore the Old Etonian colours of blue stripes on black. Glancing at the tie for a moment, he seemed to change his mind, and turned it over. The reversed side was patterned with the Old Harrovian colours – which he knotted at his throat. And all the time whistling contentedly under his breath.

'So just put your skates on, and push off,' said Fernworthy.

'Like he said,' grated Coker. 'Move it, creep!'

There was a bedside table : a solid thing of walnut and ormolu upon which stood the telephone. Freddie Carruthers picked up the latter and laid it carefully upon the bed. Then, in one swift movement, he turned, his right hand slicing down. The heel of his palm struck the centre of the table top and continued downwards. The table fell to the floor in two halves.

He was still smiling when he turned to look into their shocked faces.

'That's the way it is, chaps,' he drawled. 'Freddie's in the driving seat now, and running the show. String along with Freddie, and there'll be something in it for you. Get in my way, and I'll tread on you. I'll tell you this, chaps : nothing's getting between Freddie and those lovely millions, least of all – ' he spat out the words – 'least of all a goddamned cripple and a muscle-bound faggot !'

Freddie was holding forth. Freddie in his Old Harrovian tie, shooting his cuffs to show his crested gold links, flashing his crested signet ring, hitching his trousers to reveal his hand-made half-boots. No more the cafeteria. They had lunched in a Soho restaurant that was frequented by the expense account set, and Freddie had had nine native oysters ('A dozen's too many, chaps, and half a dozen too few') and a twelve-ounce steak, done blue ('Just ask the chef chappie to wave a lighted match over it'); and had just settled the bill by means of a credit card that he offered the head waiter for selection from many such in a neat black crocodile case. Fernworthy wondered how long it took for credit companies to catch up with him.

The others had not eaten much, and Angela scarcely anything. She was wearing dark glasses, and betrayed herself by a tremor of her hand as she raised the coffee cup to her lips. Fernworthy's heart went out to her. He swore to himself that, if he had a gun handy, he would have shot Freddie where he sat.

The object of Fernworthy's fury, all unaware of the hazard, took a sip of his *fine* and resumed his holding-forth.

'Notwithstanding the excellence of Angie's prospectus,' he said, 'I hold her basic premise entirely to question. Maximalizing the product is all fine and large, but it is in the *collection* of the profits that we are going to come unstuck. Consider : today's *Epicure* contains no less than two thousand, one hundred and thirty-six offers, of

which I have calculated – ' he consulted the back of
a used envelope which he took from his waistcoat
pocket – 'of which I have calculated about three hundred
to be top bidders. The way it's working out, m'dears,
we are faced with the daunting prospect of literally
selling Uncle Karl piecemeal. Every item going to a
separate buyer. Can you *imagine* the hazard involved
in all those separate pick-ups? I tell you, it's not on.'

'And what do you propose?' demanded Fernworthy
coldly.

'I'm glad you asked me that, Ed,' responded Freddie.
'And I'll give you the straight answer. We junk that list
of offers from the small ads in the *Epicure* and sit
tight.'

'Sit tight – for what?' asked Fernworthy.

'For one of the big boys to make an offer,' said
Freddie. 'Or both.'

'Russia and China?'

'Who else, laddie?'

'They've showed no signs of interest yet,' said Fernworthy.

'They will. Give 'em time.' Freddie yawned, drew
from his waistcoat pocket a gold half-hunter watch on
the end of a slender gold chain, consulted it. 'It's been
a hard day,' he said, 'and I'm for a couple of hours in
beddie-byes. Coming, wifie dear?'

Angela picked up her handbag, and Fernworthy saw
her fingers tremble. But her eyes were inscrutable behind
the dark glasses. He rose when she did, and Coker followed suit.

'Keep in touch, chaps,' said Freddie. 'Best phone in to
Angie and me every morning. For instructions, you know.
As soon as the big boys come up with their offer, we'll
all get together and contrive a safe means to make the
pick-up. Okay? Come on, Angie sweet. Up the wooden

hill to Bedfordshire.'

Angela had not spoken throughout the entire meal. Fernworthy and Coker watched her follow the tall figure of her husband out of the restaurant door. They then sat down.

'I'm going to have a large whisky,' said Fernworthy. 'Join me?'

'Yeah!' Coker drove one big fist into the palm of his other hand. 'When I think of that bastard . . . !'

'Two large whiskies, waiter,' said Fernworthy.

'We're gonna have to kill him,' said Coker in a strangled voice. 'You know that, Ed. We're gonna have to kill him!'

'Yes, Jay,' said Fernworthy. 'But – how?'

'We'll find a way,' said Coker. 'Just so's we're both of the same mind, Ed.'

'We think as one, Jay.'

'When I think of that bastard, Ed. When I think of that sneering bastard. And that swell girl. That sweet and lovely kid.' He drove his fist, again, into the palm of his other hand.

'You're right, Jay.'

'You're darned right I'm right!'

Silence – and then :

'Jay, what he said about you – you know?'

'He had me figured, Ed. Sure, I'm gay. So what?'

'But – I thought – well, you were with Angela, at her place that night . . .'

'Hell, I just went round to fix her spin-drier in the kitchen.'

Silence.

'And Mrs Ducane, Jay? What about Eunice?'

Coker shrugged. 'She needs me, Ed. She just needs me.'

III

A WEEK WENT by. In the course of that time, the *Daily Epicure* ran extra pages to accommodate the number of small ads that continued to pour in from all over the world. Fernworthy kept a tally of the bids; broke them down into countries of origin, types of bidder. But no sign from Red China or the USSR: as far as they were concerned, the kidnapping of their principal begetter's remains might never have happened. NATO called off the emergency. The USA reluctantly conceded that, after all, the British Government's writ might not be deemed to have extended to the private grave of a long-dead alien. The topic slipped from the front pages of the world to half-columns on feature pages. But still the small ads continued to come in.

Fernworthy saw the point. It came to him – as so often all his best insights did – while cleaning his teeth in front of the bathroom mirror. He rang Angela's number straight away: demanded, and got, an immediate, emergency meeting of all four interested parties that evening in the South Kensington flat.

They sat around in the front room, which was Angela's drawing-room. She was still wearing dark glasses. Freddie was in dark grey clerical worsted, hand-sewn; his tie Eton-side outwards. Jay Coker, in his Oxford T-shirt, sat punching his fist into the palm of his other hand.

'Proceed, laddie,' said Freddie amiably.

Fernworthy drew a deep breath and discovered that he was nervous. He glanced down at the *aide-mémoire* that he had composed that afternoon.

'I am of the opinion,' he said. Then, clearing his

throat to get a clearer, firmer tone, he went on : 'I am of the opinion that we are not going to receive an offer from either of the major Communist powers, Russia or China, and that our best option is to accept the highest bids from those we have already received.'

'Clarify, laddie,' drawled Freddie. 'Upon what evidence do you base that assumption ?'

'Only upon the lack of response from Russia and China.'

'It isn't a lot, laddie. What else ?'

'Inference.'

'You have the floor, laddie. Shoot.'

Fernworthy took another glance at his *aide-mémoire*, and said : 'The big Red powers don't want Marx's remains at any price. Why? Because he's an embarrassment. A lot of water has flowed under a lot of bridges since the Russian Revolution and all that happened after, both in that country and in China. Marx represents the primitive orthodoxy of Communism; whereas a lot of revisionism has taken place down the years. For us to offer the bones of Marx to the men in the Kremlin, it's like – well, it's like offering the bones of St Peter to the Methodists, to carry around the streets in procession, with candles and incense. It's like asking a young Levantine Jew from Nazareth, in his grubby caftan and *burnous*, for sherry at the manor house after Sunday matins in the village church. Total embarrassment all round. Communism, like all religions, has moved on; hardened into Establishment. The big men at the Kremlin and in Peking don't want to be reminded about Marx too much. He made a lot of fairly specific promises – as did the young Jew from Nazareth and St Peter – that have been fumbled and forgotten by the sleek characters in the bureaux. We won't get any offers from those characters. For them, Marx is just a name from the past.'

'But what about the others?' It was Angela who interposed the question. She was not wearing the dark glasses, and her luminous, dark eyes were alight with intelligence. 'What about the small ads?' She tapped the copy of the *Epicure* that she was holding.

'The people who want Marx,' said Fernworthy, 'are – with the exception of rich collectors – little people. Members of small collectives in China and Cuba. Downtrodden workers in state factories and sweatshops behind the Iron Curtain. Idealists belonging to Marxist revival parties in Southern Italy and Latin America. People for whom Marx is a vision of a future that might lie beyond their present misery; the Messiah whose promises might never come true, but whose relics can be paraded, with incense and candles, or drums and slogans, to keep hope alive. That's what I think.' He sat down and found to his surprise that his hands were trembling.

'He's right,' said Angela.

'I'll buy it,' said Coker.

Freddie shot his cuffs, examined his polished fingernails for a few moments, and said : 'Inconvenient though it may be, I am inclined to believe that friend Fernworthy has hit upon the truth of it. Question is, where do we go from here?'

'The answer's in this late edition of the *Epicure*,' said Angela. 'I don't suppose any of you have been right through the latest list, but there is an ad which is quite different from the rest. Look . . .' She first passed the paper – pointedly – to Fernworthy.

He read the paragraph under her finger :

The Southern Italian C.P. (Marxist-Leninist) offer to act as *honest brokers* to those holding the remains of

Karl Marx, in their dealings with would-be purchasers. Phone . . .

There was a London telephone number. Even as Fernworthy looked up and met Angela's eyes, she reached out and dialled it on the extension in the room. She listened. Held the receiver out for them all to hear.

'Engaged,' she said.

'With an ad like this,' said Coker, who had just read it, 'that phone will be busy for evermore with every nut in Britain and every two-bit crook who wants to muscle in on the act.'

Freddie Carruthers looked up from reading the ad. 'This is the answer,' he said. 'We must keep ringing – all of us, day and night – till we get on to those people.'

And that was how it was left.

Fernworthy and Coker departed together. It was raining out in the streets, and they walked swiftly to the underground station, closely huddled together.

'We're getting close to it, Ed,' said Coker. 'The pay-off.'

'I feel that, too, Jay,' said Fernworthy.

'We've gotta move fast, if we're going to fix that bastard Carruthers. Come the pay-off, he'll double-cross the three of us and disappear.'

'Yes, he will.'

'Ed, do you still want to go through with it?'

'Yes, if you do, Jay.'

'Well, just to tell you I've got the stuff to do it.'

'You mean . . . ?'

'Poison. I got it from the guy who also supplied our employment cards.'

'*Poison!* Ohmygod!'

※

Next morning, Fernworthy supplied himself with a pocket full of coins and went round to the phone box on the corner, where he first called Angela's number. It was she who answered, and her voice sounded thick and husky.

'I haven't managed to raise these people yet,' she said. 'And I've started a lousy cold.'

'They've been engaged all the time?'

'Yes.'

'Take a rest, Angela,' he said. 'Go back to bed. I'll try for an hour or so. Are you sure you'll be all right? Is – you-know-who with you?'

'He's gone out, thank heaven. I don't think I could stomach that bastard *and* a cold !'

'You won't have to,' he muttered savagely at his reflection in the mirror.

'What did you say?'

'Nothing. I'll ring off now, Angela. Look after yourself. See you.'

The short exchange with the object of his dearest passions steeled Fernworthy's nerve to contemplating the issue that he had spent a sleepless night in avoiding : the killing of Freddie Carruthers. The inflection of her voice – the weariness and the self-loathing that told of what she was suffering at the hands of that sneering brute to whom she was married – drove him into a frenzy of hatred, so that he imagined himself choking the life out of her tormentor, fingers clenched about his reversible old school tie, screaming down into his contused, dying face. You'll never lay your filthy hands on that beautiful body again, you stinking swine. I'll – I'll . . .

He looked up, panting, to see that two would-be users of the phone box – an elderly man and a stout young woman – were gazing through the windows at him in amazement and affront. He assembled a sickly smile, put a coin in the slot and began dialling. On the third try, he got the ringing tone. A Latin-sounding voice answered almost immediately.

'All right, Mr Caller, you're the tenth this morning. I'll cut it short by telling you that the British Home Office have co-operated by giving us the text of the message that the kidnappers left in the grave. Tell me the first line of the text and we're in business. Otherwise, ring off and get lost.'

'I have a copy of the text with me,' said Fernworthy, who had come prepared. He took it from out of his pocket and laid it down on top of a phone book.

'Okay. Shoot.'

'The first line reads: "It is true that liberty is precious — so precious that it must be rationed." That's a quotation from . . .'

'From Lenin. You don't have to play schoolmaster with me, mister. Yes, we're in business. Listen . . .'

'No, you listen!' said Fernworthy. 'We'll be in touch with you later with instructions. Give me another number to call you at. This one's a dead duck.'

'Good thinking, mister. I have one all ready for you.'

Fernworthy wrote down the number and rang off.

Another call to South Kensington established that Angela had indeed gone back to bed with her cold: she spoke from her bedside extension; told him that Freddie was due back at any time; yes, it was good news that he had made contact with the honest brokers; and Jay Coker had phoned to say he wanted to see him, Fernworthy, and he was to go straight back home, where the American would be waiting for him. And now leave her to her misery, concluded Angela.

Coker was leaning on the gate outside Fernworthy's place. They entered together. The big American seemed unimpressed to hear of his companion's success on the telephone; instead, he appeared pensive, withdrawn. The reason for this became apparent when he took from the pocket of his jeans a small green glass bottle and placed it on the kitchen table.

'That,' he said succinctly, 'is *it*!'

'The – poison?' breathed Fernworthy.

Coker nodded. 'The guy said it was pretty fast acting. First symptoms within four hours. Unconsciousness and coma soon after. Process irreversible. Good night, sweet prince.'

'How're we going to give it to him?'

'The man said – he was most informative – that the classic method is the convivial bottle method. Leastways, it's how the top hit men, those who use poison, do it. You go around to the guy's place with a bottle, which the two of you proceed to drink. All pals together. If he had any suspicion that you were going to slip something into his glass, he'd be fooled completely. Because you don't. You wait till there are only two drinks left in the bottle . . .'

'Then you slip the poison into the bottle!'

'Right. My, you're quick. You let him pour out the last two drinks, yours and his . . .'

'But you take care not to drink yours!'

'Again, right!'

'It's fiendishly simple. Fiendishly clever. Like Columbus's egg.'

'It's a one-man job,' said Coker. 'With the convivial bottle method.'

'Which of us is going to do it?'

Coker took a fifty-pence piece from his pocket and showed both sides. 'You call.'

The coin spun into the air, winking silver lights in the sunshine through the kitchen window.

'Heads I go,' said Fernworthy.

The Sovereign's head lay in Coker's palm. Fernworthy felt the short hairs at the back of his neck pucker and bristle, and his flesh crawled all over, describing the whole shape of his body, even his missing hand.

'It's your show, boss,' whispered Coker.

They spent the day together, bringing in a Chinese take-away lunch, and going to a cinema in the afternoon. On the way back, Fernworthy rang South Kensington, and when Freddie answered, told him he wanted to come round and discuss the arrangements to be made with the honest brokers. Freddie told him to come at eight. From the off-licence on the corner of Fernworthy's road, they bought a bottle of good malt whisky, guaranteed ten years old.

At six-thirty, they had bacon and eggs and canned lager in Fernworthy's kitchen.

Coker said: 'What are you going to do with your money, Ed?'

'Haven't given it a great deal of thought,' said Fernworthy. 'Apart from buying me independence, the means to travel, a few very nice pictures, it will probably pose quite a problem.' What about the portals of hymen? he asked himself, but added aloud: 'What shall you do with yours, Jay? Go back to the States and make a big splash?'

Coker shrugged, drained the last of his lager can. 'I aim to help out a few folks,' he said. 'Folks like Eunice and her kids. Dunno whether I'll do it here or the States. Doesn't really make a helluva difference. There's plenny in both places who need the help.'

'What kind of help, Jay?' asked Fernworthy.

Coker's guileless eyes widened with surprise. 'For Pete's sake, Ed, you've seen Eunice and her set-up. Don't you get the scenario? That dame needs a nurse and bodyguard in attendance day and night. You leave her standing outside a store while you dart in to get a pack of cigarettes; she's got herself pregnant by the time you get out. If I don't take the social security money right out of her hands, it goes on pot and hash. Eunice is a full-time job, and I've had to neglect her of late. And, man, there's a thousand Eunices, straight and gay, right here in the teeming heart of this great city.'

'And you're going to start a home for them?'

'Something like that. Yeah, some kind of home, I guess.'

'You make my hedonism sound very cheap, Jay.'

'You're going to have to work hard for that hedonism, man. Starting at eight tonight.'

It was the sort of summer night that parts of London – and South Kensington is one of them – do very well; with a hint of blossom from behind garden walls; a scent of rain-washed streets; a lightest touch of the exotic, agarbathies and curry powder; people speaking very quietly, and the unlikely sound of a lawnmower. It was still very warm, though the sun was down below the rooftops of Cromwell Road, where Australian bed-sitters dream of home and the Outback.

Bottle of whisky under his arm, Fernworthy marched to his date with destiny. In his left hand, clenched within his pocket, he held the small bottle that was to reduce Carruthers to unconsciousness, coma and oblivion. He had practised the motions of removing the stopper and inverting it over the neck of a whisky bottle, one-handed. It could be done in the time it takes the other party to, say, reach down and pick up a fallen cigarette lighter.

He rang the bell of Angela's place. Freddie opened the door to him.

'*Bonsoir*, friend Fernworthy,' he cried. With a faint

sense of relief, Fernworthy realized that his victim was already rather drunk. 'Come in, laddie. What's this? An offering? Ten-year malt, no less. Egad, you are indeed welcome, friend Fernworthy.'

'How is – er – Angela?' asked Fernworthy, with an anxious glance towards the bedroom door. He and Coker had firmly decided that the attempt was to be postponed if she was up and about.

'Not well, poor little dear,' said Freddie. 'In view of which, I have abandoned my connubial bed in favour of the sofa in the sitting-room. Now – two clean glasses and we will proceed to sample this excellent ten-year malt.'

Another plus, thought Fernworthy. The victim's symptoms would not commence in Angela's bed, nor the ensuing unconsciousness, coma and dissolution.

'I hope she'll be better in the morning,' he said. Well enough, at least, to open the door to Coker and himself when they came to collect the remains for disposal . . .

'Let us drink to that, laddie,' said Freddie, handing Fernworthy a brimming whisky glass and raising the other to his lips. 'Chin-chin and tally-ho.'

'Your very good health,' murmured Fernworthy, glancing at the level of the whisky remaining in the bottle. Despite the generous measures, it still seemed a long way to go. He should have brought only a half-bottle.

'And now,' said Freddie, 'to business.' He settled himself in an armchair and waved to Fernworthy to do likewise. 'So we are in contact with the self-styled honest brokers. How did he sound, the chappie you spoke to?'

'An English-speaking Italian,' said Fernworthy. 'And no fool, by the sound of him. If his associates are all of that ilk, I'd say we can do business with them.'

'Excellent, excellent,' said Freddie, taking a pull of

his whisky, and then dabbing his moustache with a red silk handkerchief which had been fluttering in his breast pocket like a battle ensign. He was in Glenurquhart tweeds and his tie was Eton-side out. 'Now, as to method of payment. I suggest the money should be deposited in a numbered Swiss bank account.'

Fernworthy experienced a prickling of intense interest, which could not entirely be accounted for by the neat whisky he had drunk.

'Do you know, that's exactly what I'd decided,' he cried.

'Great minds, my dear fellow, great minds.'

'A bank in – say – Chiasso,' said Fernworthy.

'Which is conveniently near to the Italian border,' said Freddie. 'And allows Milanese businessmen to pop over with the odd suitcase of unaccounted lire.'

'But I don't think we hand over the goods in Chiasso,' said Fernworthy. 'The two ends of the operation should be kept well apart.'

'Though one of us will have to be in Chiasso, to check that the money has been paid in, before we hand over the merchandise. Don't forget that, laddie.'

'Quite,' said Fernworthy. 'And I suggest that we distance the hand-over even further from Chiasso than Milan. What about – Rome?'

'Rome will be excellent,' said Freddie. 'Pass me your glass, laddie. This is thirsty business, and I must say I am enjoying working with you tremendously. We see eye to eye perfectly.'

'Thank you – er – Freddie,' said Fernworthy, accepting another bumper of whisky. He was really quite enjoying their conversation. The planning had a keen element of excitement, and he was obliged to slip his hand into his pocket and make contact with the poison bottle, in order to bring his mind back to the needs of the hour.

Freddie took a deep draught of his whisky. 'We could find that the line of communication between Chiasso and Rome is a mite on the long side,' he said.

'The distance scarcely matters,' said Fernworthy. 'Near or far, we could have our fellow in Chiasso standing there with egg on his face trying to report through on a busy line.'

'We need alternative communication centres,' said Freddie. 'With a main centre constantly manned through-out the operation.'

'And not a hotel bedroom,' said Fernworthy. 'Hotel switchboards are notoriously inefficient. Besides, the operators can listen in. And frequently do.'

'I've got it!' said Freddie. 'A public call box in a café. That's the ticket. We'll have Angela monopolize it for the duration of the job.'

'Yes, that would do the trick,' said Fernworthy.

'That's settled then,' said Freddie. 'Cheers, laddie! You will instruct your friend, the honest broker, that he is to obtain the monies from those bidders whom you designate. He is then to open a numbered Swiss bank account, on our behalf, at a bank in Chiasso. The monies having been paid into the account, we will then pass over the merchandise in Rome. That is the broad picture of the operation as I see it. The details – the tim-ing of the hand-over, the means by which we assure our-selves that the money is indeed in the account and that we are able to withdraw it – can be left till later. This really is most excellent malt, laddie.'

Ten o'clock. As far as Fernworthy could gauge – and it was not easy, the way his eyes were acting up – there were two more drinks apiece in the bottle. One more slug like this one – he gagged on a mouthful, to keep pace with his companion – and he would have to contrive a small diversion, in order to allow himself time and opportunity to add the poison . . .

Freddie was talking. Freddie, who had started drinking earlier in the evening, yet who had shown excellent form all the way down the bottle, had taken a sudden turn for the worse. He was now becoming maudlin, even lachrymose. He was on the subject of his childhood upbringing; specifically, at the moment, on his father . . .

'My old man,' he said. 'My dear old dad, now he was a bit of a rogue. A love – a loveable old rogue. You know wha' I mean? My old man, he made a good living by throwing himself in front of Rolls-Royces and settling for damages out of court.'

'Very – precarious way of earning a living,' ventured Fernworthy.

'He didn't give a damn about the risk!' cried Freddie. 'Just so he provided for his family. We never went without. Never! Always plenty to eat on the table. Stout shoes for all of us. Two weeks' holiday every year – buckets and spades, sand-castles, the lot! And as soon as things started to get a bit tight, as soon as the old piggy bank ceased to rattle – wham! – straight under the next Rolls-Royce went my old man. Marvellous old bugger. Marvellous.' He dabbed his streaming eyes with the red silk handkerchief. 'They don't come like him any more. When they made my old man, they threw away the mould.'

Fernworthy closed his eyes, but the room went round at such an alarming rate that he snapped them open hastily.

'Did – did your father pur-pursue his hazardous calling to the end?' he asked.

'That he did, laddie,' said Freddie. 'That he did. By a cruel stroke of fate, a chance of blind tragedy, the dear old chap happened upon a lady driver. Mark you, I am not shu-suggesting that the fair sex possess less inherent competence than the rest of us; but I am speaking of those far-off days before the war, before the days of driving tests, when any twit with a cheque book could march into a showroom, buy a car and drive off with it, learning along the way. The lady in question was one such. In addition she was a lady of her time – which is to say she saw fit to affect a certain hysteria in tight corners that a modern miss would be ashamed to display. When she realized that she had driven over my old man, she lost her head. Slammed into reverse. Went over him again. That did for poor Dad.' He was crying quite unashamedly.

'I'm terribly sorry, Freddie,' said Fernworthy.

'We didn't starve!' cried Freddie. 'Mother took over where Dad left off. No, she didn't throw herself under Rolls-Royces, she took in washing. Do you hear that, laddie? My poor old mum took in washing. That surprises you, hey?'

'I confess,' said Fernworthy, 'that it does – it does.' He must remember to slip in the poison before Freddie poured out the last two glasses . . .

'I've got a confession to make, laddie,' said his intended victim. His voice sank to a whisper. 'I didn't go to Eton. No, nor Harrow either. Wha' do you think of that?'

Fernworthy sketched a doubting gesture, and nearly fell off the edge of his chair. He then addressed himself to taking hold of the poison bottle, in preparation for the big moment.

'Nah, I went to a boarding school in Norfolk,' said

Freddie. 'It wash-wasn't even a public school, though it dearly would like to've been. It was run by a boring old fart named Eagles, who hanged himself in rather suspicious circumstances in 'forty-three, or it may have been 'forty-four, and the site of the old school is now covered with rural council dwellings, or they may have sown salt there – ' he was far away in his lachrymose meanderings, eyes closed – 'I was Captain of Cricket by reason of the fact that I was the only boy who possessed a cricket bat and two pads; and I was Senior Latin Scholar because I was the only boy doing Latin . . .' His voice trailed off.

Fumblingly, Fernworthy uncorked the poison and directed his hand towards the open whisky bottle that stood on the table before him. His hand was no problem; the problem was so to bring his eyes into focus, and so to work them in conjunction one with the other, that it was possible to determine if the neck of the poison bottle was before or behind the neck of the whisky bottle.

Without opening his eyes, Freddie droned on : 'Fate bought me a second class ticket for my journey through life. I wash not involved in this choice. At the age of eighteen, I tore up this second class ticket. Sinsh then, laddie, Freddie hash travelled through life first class de luxe. How's about another lil' drink, laddie?'

Fernworthy's hand had just returned to his pocket with the empty poison bottle, as his victim reached out and poured whisky into both their glasses, overspilling the last drops and shaking out the dregs. Fernworthy closed his eyes and sighed with relief. He was instantly overcome with such violent nausea that he all but threw up. The room began to spin round at an alarming rate, and everything receded to a vast distance. Opening his eyes, he saw that a perfect stranger in a Glenurquhart suit was draining a glass of whisky, and calling upon him to do likewise. There seemed no point in offending the fellow, who, later, might be able to give him some clue as to who he was and where he was.

He took the proffered glass, aimed it towards his mouth – and drank it down.

He woke in blinding sunlight, which was like the great light of the Gulf of Sorrento that flooded the hospital ward on the day that he woke up, and the young nursing nun had told him he must have fortitude, then broke it to him that they had taken off his right hand. He had wept then, and felt ill enough to weep now. His head was bursting.

He sat up. Freddie Carruthers was asleep in the armchair opposite, with his head lolling back against the cushions, hands folded across his waistcoat front, snoring quietly.

It was broad daylight and – he squinted against the strong sunlight and focused on the clock on the chimney-piece – past nine o'clock. He – and his companion – must have been asleep for all of ten hours.

Ten hours!

He leapt to his feet, and was instantly assaulted by a stab of pain behind the eyes. It quickly went, leaving a dull ache.

The poison!

The empty whisky bottle was on the table. With it were two glasses, his own and Freddie's . . .

Both empty!

A frenzied search through his pockets produced the unstoppered poison bottle, also empty.

Options, options . . .

Either he had managed to put the poison in the last of the whisky, or he had not. Either, in his drunken stupor, he had then joined his victim in the last, fatal glass, or he had not. As to external evidence, he was still alive and — save for a cracking hangover — free of fatal symptoms ten hours after the event. Furthermore, the man opposite looked the very picture of inebriated good health.

One more clue : there was a streak of dampness on the upper part of his trouser-leg, in line with his left-hand trouser pocket. Bending to sniff at it, he detected a faint and alien odour. It was likely to be the poison, he decided : split in one go as he had drunkenly fumbled out the stopper prior to upending the — then empty — bottle into the remains of the whisky. His clumsiness had spared the life of Freddie Carruthers, and incidentally his own.

Suddenly, it felt tremendously good to be alive, strangely exhilarating, also, not to be a murderer; but only a failed, incompetent murderer. He brushed a fly off Freddie's head *en passant* for the door; glanced longingly towards Angela's bedroom when he reached the hallway; went out into the morning.

South Kensington looked a treat to the eye and the air smelt like wine. Despite the frightful taste in his mouth, he felt as hungry as he had ever felt in his life. So he went in search of somewhere for a slap-up breakfast of fried eggs, sausages, bacon, and all the trimmings.

Allegro Vivace

I

FERNWORTHY'S MARKED aversion to flying stemmed partly from a tendency to claustrophobia and partly from a fastidiousness about the lavatory arrangements. He spent a thoroughly uncomfortable journey from Heathrow to Leonardo da Vinci, and was only cheered by the presence of Angela Carruthers at his side and the first glimpse of the Eternal City glowing distantly under the wing of the Alitalia DC9 as it banked to make its approach.

He and Angela had travelled alone; Jay Coker and Freddie Carruthers were already in Chiasso, attending to that end of the programme. Freddie was to join them in Rome in a couple of days' time, leaving Coker in Switzerland to finalize the operation there. Fernworthy rejoiced that he would have Angela to himself for two whole days. He could have wished to have made a more promising start to the intimacy, but had to acknowledge that he was not at his best in aeroplanes.

Angela said: 'You must know Rome quite well.'

'I was here for a while during my pre-university year,' said Fernworthy. He recalled that it had been, for him, a most rewarding time – both financially and culturally. The pickings in the crowded museums, churches and art galleries of the Eternal City had exceeded anything that either he or Arthur Ealing had been used to as schoolboys in the byways of Uppingham. 'I must take you to the Villa D'Este in Tivoli,' he said.

'There's an adorable little picture by Fragonard of the Villa D'Este,' she said.

'Yes,' said Fernworthy. She really was a most delightfully well-informed creature, quite apart from being the very epitome of beauty. 'It's in the Wallace Collection. I fell in love with the Villa D'Este, thanks to Fragonard, before I ever set eyes on the terraces and the water gardens.'

'I shall look forward to your taking me there,' said Angela.

Any further exploitation of the Villa D'Este theme was cut short by a request on the part of the stewardess to fasten seat-belts in readiness for landing, and together they watched the Roman campagna slide past below : the tree-lined roads where patient donkeys plodded; tillers in the dry fields; the crumbling stonework of farmhouses that had been old when Columbus sailed; Cinzano posters; motor scooters.

I will make the most of the opportunity, thought Fernworthy. The like of it may never come again. I have two days at least – maybe more, for there was a lot of work for Jay and Freddie to do in Switzerland. They had gone there by the Continental express train (a far cry, that, from the old Orient Express famed in song and story), which makes a stop at Chiasso. With them they had taken what all four had by then come to refer to as 'the merchandise' – for who searches baggage on continental trains nowadays? The kidnappers were calling the rules, and the honest brokers were obeying implicitly. Jay's and Freddie's task in Chiasso was manifold : physically to choose, by reason of accessibility, the bank in which the deposit was to be made; to test the telephone communications between Chiasso and Rome; and to give final instructions to the honest brokers when everything had been tried and found to be foolproof.

Yes, he thought. They'll be lucky to get all that done in two days. More like the week-end before her cad of a husband arrives in Rome to resume his conjugal rights. He cast a sidelong glance at Angela. She really did look spiffing in that black and white print dress with the dainty black kid gloves, matching shoes and handbag. It was an outfit that had cost a pretty penny, as had his new, off-the-peg suit in lightweight navy. He had financed the entire Italian operation, including new outfits and baggage for the team; financed it from the sale — to the same off-Bond Street shop where the Boudin of Trouville still languished, unsold (but, hopefully, not for long) — of his undoubted Meissonnier dragoon.

Three days, call it four, to complete the first seduction of his life. Was it possible? The desire was there, right enough; and he had arrived on terms with Angela such as he had never achieved with any other woman. They laughed at the same things, approved of the same breeds of dog, objected to the English abroad; mutually disliked airline food, but approved of unlimited champagne on a first-class ticket. Was it enough, though, to pave the way to her bed? Only time would tell.

They passed over a red pantiled roof of a farmhouse, a battery of landing lights standing like Martians in a field of plough, a perimeter road. The wheels bumped, the engines shrieked into reverse. He looked down to find that her hand was in his, and was surprised to realize that this immensely cool and self-contained woman was a nervous flyer.

They hired a self-drive Fiat and went to Tivoli, which is only 27 kilometres out of Rome. The little square was packed with touring buses and milling with camera-hung folk who reminded him of the days when he was working the 'discipline'; he ran a professional eye over a perspir-

ing German and put him down for an industrialist with
a fat billroll. Ah, those dead days of yore!

'It's dreadfully hot,' said Angela. 'Let's get near those
lovely fountains in the water garden.'

She was unimpressed by the Villa itself, which dates
from 1550, is rather severe, and not to everyone's taste
in Renaissance architecture. Privately, Fernworthy dis-
approved of some of the interior frescoes, which he con-
sidered he could have done better himself. But, if the Villa
was a let-down, not so the water gardens.

'Oh, Ed, what a delight!' cried Angela, clapping
her hands with all the unselfconscious abandonment of a
little girl, and earning for herself a row of wistful stares
from a passing posse of pale seminarists in long black
soutanes.

Two tiers of stone lions' heads – there must have been
a hundred in a line – belched crystal water into a long
trough, that was set along a tree-shaded path; this fed
other streams and waterways, rills and runlets, that
descended the steep slope on which the garden was set.
The sounds of moving water were all about them –
the only sounds to be heard: merry gurgling, tinkle-
tinkle, drip-drip, gushing libation, and – above it all –
the lordly hiss of the great fountains at the base, that rose
tree-high and reflected the sun in a million droplets.

'The most impressive part,' said Fernworthy, 'is the
Water Organ, and it's best seen from above. Come
on.'

He took her hand. Hand-in-hand, they ran down the
steps, where the torrents of water swept past in time-
worn gutterings on both sides; till they came to a path
overhung with dark greenery, where, all alone as they
were, Fernworthy was tempted to take hold of Angela
and kiss her. The temptation made him tremble, but was
soon past. They came out into the sunshine again, and

were standing on a balustraded terrace high above a complex of fountains, waterfalls and lichened stonework : the Water Organ. Every sound of water, every note that it can make in movement, burst upon their ears.

He looked at her profile, pink-brown with the day's sun. Her lustrous eyes were half-closed, her lips parted to show the whiteness of her teeth, the slight irregularity of her incisors. Her hands were resting on the balustrade. The subtle curve of her bosom, rising and falling with her slight breathlessness from running, so entranced him that, without a moment's pause for reflection, he was constrained to offer it a slight caress.

She turned to face him, eyes wide and surprised.

'Well – what now?' she demanded flatly.

'I – I'm awfully sorry,' stammered Fernworthy. 'I really don't know what came over me. Please – please forget what I did.'

A moment's silence, and she said contemptuously : 'I was mistaken in you. It never occurred to me that you were one of the dirty mac brigade.'

She turned on her heel and walked swiftly back the way they had come.

'Angela ! Wait – please !' He set off after her, and she quickened her step.

The line of seminarists were straggling towards them along the tree-shaded path, and their longing eyes turned in succession upon the young woman who fled past them. There was shaking of heads when they saw Fernworthy stumbling after her as fast as his short wind and long-unexercised legs would carry him.

She beat him hands down to the steps that led up to the Villa and the exit beyond. He panted out into the town square in time to see the Fiat doing a U-turn under the nose of an astonished policeman, set off the wrong way down a one-way street and vanish from their sight.

The policeman, tiring of blowing his whistle to the empty air, produced a notebook and demanded to know if the *signora* was his, Fernworthy's, wife. That much Italian Fernworthy understood.

It seemed prudent, all things considering, to deny that he even knew her.

It was six o'clock and apéritif time. Half Rome was sitting out in street cafés, and Fernworthy chose a table that was unoccupied and in the shade. It was round the corner from St Peter's Square, and the high walls of the Vatican City cast a long shadow across the busy, narrow street.

He ordered a large Pernod on the rocks, in the hope that the tang of the aniseed would make some inroads upon the sour taste in his mouth. Worry – any sort of worry – tended to give him heartburn and dyspepsia. He had been worried sick all the afternoon, all through the interminable, hot drive back to the city in the municipal bus, with a stout lady in black bombasine standing on his feet, a thin individual with a squint blowing halitosis in his face, and a child in arms wailing over all.

He had made of himself a total and irremediable fool in Angela's eyes. 'Dirty macintosh brigade' – that about summed it up. He supposed that he qualified for the title : the long-past visit to the *Folies Bergère* had decidedly been of the dirty mac persuasion, likewise the disastrous encounter with the Florentine tart. He downed half of the Pernod, enjoying the sensation of the aromatic spirit straining its cool way into his mouth through the jingling ice cubes. With a pang of self-pity, he speculated on the ill-chance that had brought him to his present pass, and at his time of life.

Flagging the waiter for another fill-up, he decided

that it was the 'discipline' that had been his downfall. At a time when he might have been having experiences with girls of his own age and class – as, for instance, at Cambridge – he had been almost wholly absorbed – apart from his formal studies – in the business of picking other people's pockets. By the time he was thirty, he had been set in his way: a confirmed celibate, but with a leery eye for a female shape – in short, a dirty mac man.

Nor had his facility for absorbing the contents of other people's pockets been a bar, merely, to his development in the sexual area. On his Cambridge academic record, he could have followed his artistic bent and become a writer, an art historian, perhaps (he had too much honesty to consider that his talent as a painter would ever have got him anywhere); but his skilful right hand had removed any need for effort in any other direction. Furthermore, till his encounter with Jay Coker and the resulting collaboration with the team, he had never before formed any relationship with either man or woman – excepting only Arthur Ealing, and when that would-be aviator had perished in the wreckage of his Gypsy Moth it had been like losing an identical twin.

He emptied his glass, sighed, and looked up into the scrubbed, shy face of a young nun. A very young nun; she could scarcely have been more than sixteen, presumably a novice; and her coif was far from clean, and her habit rusty green with age – presumably handed down.

She was holding out her hand.

'Yes?' asked Fernworthy, bemused.

'*Mi scusi, signor.*'

'Oh, I see,' said Fernworthy. 'You're collecting. Here, let's see what we've got in the way of change.' He dipped his hand into his pocket and came out with a pile of small coin, which he put in the child-nun's not too clean palm. 'Er – what are you collecting for, sister?'

'*Mi scusi, signor? Non comprendo.*'

With a great deal of difficulty, he elicited that the pathetic little novice was collecting for orphans.

'Orphans. Ah, yes. Very commendable. Good evening to you, sister.'

He rose at her departure, bowing slightly, and discovered that the Pernod had rendered him unsteady on his feet.

'I find that incident outrageously paradoxical,' said a voice.

The speaker was sitting alone at the table adjacent to Fernworthy's, and had so far only presented his back. Turning, he revealed himself as a man of middle years, with a shrewd, dark-eyed countenance of vaguely – or so it seemed to Fernworthy – Balkan cut. Magyar, perhaps. He was dressed neatly in a suit of unseasonably heavy material and smelt ever so faintly of mothballs. He was drinking – Fernworthy took note – whisky.

'Indeed, sir?' replied Fernworthy. 'And why do you find it paradoxical, pray?'

The other turned his chair round and presented Fernworthy with a small hand that was thickly pelted with fine black hairs from fingernails to wrist.

'The name is Obernyik,' he said. His English was very good, almost unaccented. 'Delighted to make your acquaintance.'

'How do you do. Fernworthy's my name.'

If the other was taken aback to be offered a left hand he did not show it, but shook it heartily. It was then that Fernworthy experienced a slight *frisson*. The man was a total stranger, and a foreigner. One's natural insularity whispered caution on both counts, even without allowing for the nature of the enterprise that had brought him to Rome. It might be that the fellow was bored with his own company and merely wished to pass the time with a few moments' conversation. On the other hand, it might mean something very different. Despite all, the Russians – or one of their Balkan satellites – might be showing interest in the kidnapping. The arm of the KGB was long . . .

Fernworthy shuddered again.

'As to the paradox,' said Obernyik. 'I would express it this way. You have been on the tour of the Vatican, yes?'

'Very many years ago,' said Fernworthy. 'When I was an undergraduate.'

'Ah, you are a man of education,' said the other. 'This makes my task of explanation much simpler. You will have observed the contents of the Vatican as a whole, and in part. Might one say, both in the manner Classical and in the manner Romantic.'

'You could put it that way,' conceded Fernworthy. If a KGB agent, then decidedly fanciful in his manner of address.

'As a whole,' said the other, making an embracing shape with his small, hairy hands, 'it is of dubious architectural merit, being comprised of the good, the not so good, and the downright awful. As to the contents, as to its treasures of the painters', the sculptors', the craftsmens' expertise, there is probably no place on earth to rival it. You will have observed the merest door handle. Examine the most insignificant door handle – and there are scarcely two alike. This handle will perhaps be of silver-gilt, and fashioned by an artist-craftsman in a long-gone *atelier*. It will have been modelled, in the first place, in clay; its elaborate and convoluted design the result of many long hours of patient application. Next, it will have been cast in the metal, from a mould obtained from the clay model. After which will have come the polishing and gilding. Then you have just one more Vatican door handle, unique, perfect. How much will this handle fetch today, do you think, in the antique market of Europe? A thousand dollars? Two? Three?'

Fernworthy shrugged. 'Given its provenance, you could write your own cheque, I suppose,' he said.

Obernyik spread out his hands. 'For one door handle,' he said. 'One out of thousands. And the same breath-taking care, the same artistry, has gone into the fashioning of the doors with which the handles are graced. And the furnishings of the rooms upon which these doors open. And the paintings, the sculptures and the ceramics within. Consider, my friend, the Michelangelos, the Titians and the Tintorettos. The Rubenses and the Berninis, the Rembrandts – need I go on?'

'Not really,' said Fernworthy. 'The paradox, in your mind, is that, bearing in mind the truly astronomical intrinsic value of the Vatican and its contents, the Pope has a nerve to send a little waif of a teenaged nun to hang around cafés and bars and beg for pennies, when he could sell one of his door knockers and save her the trouble for life. And a couple of hundred like her. Is that your paradox?'

Obernyik hunched his shoulders. 'Perfectly expressed, my friend,' he said. 'And do you not agree?'

'Sell up the Vatican and ease the lot of the orphaned, the poor, the destitute? Is it a very good bargain?'

'Is art more important than life?' countered the other.

'That's sophistry,' said Fernworthy. 'Sell up the Vatican in job lots, and you've gone a long way towards dismembering the Church itself. The place has taken nearly two thousand years in the assembling. Destroy it,

and the idea behind it would be forgotten in a genera-
tion.'

'Would that be a bad thing?' asked his companion
quietly.

'Maybe not entirely,' said Fernworthy. 'No one would
miss the fat prelates, the puffed-up cardinals, the place-
seeking, a lot of the mumbo-jumbo. But I tell you what
the world *would* miss out on.'

'And what is that?' asked Obernyik.

'Nervous little nuns who hang around bars and
collect pennies for orphan kids,' said Fernworthy.

The dark eyes brightened with pure pleasure, and
Obernyik clapped his hands. 'You have confounded me
entirely, my friend,' he said. 'And for that I will now
buy you a drink.'

They parted company half an hour later, Fernworthy
to return to his hotel, Obernyik to keep an appointment
for seven o'clock.

The latter walked straight across St Peter's Square,
and presented himself at the gates on the left of the
great cathedral, where a Swiss Guard in full, Michel-
angelo-styled regimentals, hearing his credentials, tapped
the butt of his halbard on the pavement and summoned
a brother Switzer in undress uniform, who escorted
Obernyik through a shady garden, where black-soutaned
minor divines conversed among gesticulating statuary and
a black African archbishop walked his Scottie on a lead;
to the echoing corridors of the palace which houses the
ancient and creakingly efficient machinery sometime
known by the name of The Holy Office. There, after
some waiting, the Switzer was permitted to whisper in the
ear of a severe cleric, who, after glancing dispassionately
at Obernyik, addressed some words into an extremely
sophisticated intercom, and upon receiving an answer

motioned the visitor to follow him. After some distance, he tapped upon a green baize door and was bidden to enter.

'Signor Obernyik, Monsignor.'

'Ask him to come in, please.'

Obernyik was ushered into a sparsely-furnished office, and a tall figure rose from behind a roll-top desk and gazed over half-moon spectacles at his entry.

'Monsignor Rietti?' asked Obernyik.

'I am he, sir. Shall we converse in English, since it is our best, common language, as I understand? Please take a seat. You are dead on time.'

'The People,' responded Obernyik, giving full value to the capital P of People, 'have waited so long that they are impatient of any delays.'

'They have certainly waited an unconscionable while for the promised world revolution,' replied the other drily. 'Would you care for a sherry?'

'No, thank you,' replied Obernyik.

'If you will excuse me, I will indulge,' said Rietti. 'Would you like a sugared almond? They are sent to me direct from Paris by one of my brothers of the Society. No? I confess to a partiality that is quite sinful in its intensity. Do you find Rome terribly hot at this time of the year? Perhaps the plains of your native country are equally arid and uncomfortable.'

Obernyik made no reply, but studied the tall figure in the black soutane and the skull cap that must surely hide a bald patch that was no man-made tonsure. He knew quite a lot about Rietti. Rietti was a Jesuit and something of a whizz-kid. Educated in England and America, tipped for high office. Some said, even Pope-material. He did not strike Obernyik very forcibly, standing there at the table by the window, pouring himself a small glass of pale straw-coloured sherry (a habit he picked up in

England, no doubt); a man in his early forties, but already grey, with ascetic lines down the cheeks and a clerical pallor. Had he ever known a woman, him and his sherry and sugared almonds?

The Jesuit sauntered back to his seat, thin hands clasped about the cut-glass, as if seeking vestigial warmth from the dry and austere wine within. He sat down, fixed his visitor with the steady gaze of clever, contemplative grey eyes.

'The Cardinal,' he said.

'Corvinus,' said Obernyik.

'We want him back,' said Rietti. 'Back in Rome.'

Obernyik nodded. 'That is why I am here.'

'Then we may hope that there is a possibility of his return? It has been a long time, Mr Obernyik.'

'Since 'forty-four,' said Obernyik. 'That was when Corvinus came back to his native land. Having left it a poor student, he returned a monsignor. Ambassador of the Pope.'

Rietti took a sip of his sherry and said: 'He was the youngest Papal nuncio ever, you know, and later became one of the youngest cardinals of this century. Your people should have allowed him to come to Rome and receive the Hat.'

'Our penal system does not permit convicted criminals to travel beyond the jurisdiction of the courts. What matter? He received his hat. He was even permitted to wear it on one occasion.'

'It was a savage sentence you gave him, Mr Obernyik,' said the Jesuit.

'He was originally sentenced for life,' replied the other. 'No question of later reprieve or parole ever entered into the courts' judgement. Now, however . . .' he spread his small hands. 'In these times of *detente*, we are able to extend small mercies towards old enemies.'

'His Eminence was never proved to have been an enemy of your People,' said Rietti. 'Not to Rome's satisfaction. Though it must be said that Rome requires an extremely searching degree of guilt. Higher, perhaps, than is required by your courts.'

'Corvinus, no matter what change of heart he may or may not have undergone in a People's prison, was a fascist when fascism ruled,' said Obernyik. 'And a consorter with the oppressors of our country.'

'He was sent as an ambassador extraordinary to the German military government of your country,' replied Rietti. 'With the specific brief to use his best influence to assist the plight of Catholics – and others – who might be suffering under the rule of the occupying power.'

Obernyik sneered. 'They sent him – a fascist!'

Rietti said: 'Corvinus was known to be of – shall we say? – ultra-conservative persuasion. What better man to treat with the Nazis? And, in this, he was extremely successful. No less than seventy-four persons – I have the figure here – were released from concentration camps and other institutes of restraint in your country. And by no means all of them were Catholics.'

'Indeed not,' conceded Obernyik. 'Some of them were even Jews. But they all had this in common : Catholics, Protestants or Jews – they were all extraordinarily rich people, with liquid assets in Switzerland!'

'That charge was made against His Eminence at his trial,' said the Jesuit. 'But was not accepted, even, by your People's judges.'

Obernyik shrugged. 'So the charge was dropped, and the prosecutor concentrated upon the matter of the three hundred and twenty-two persons who were put *into* concentration camps and other institutes of restraint at the suggestion of the influential ambassador extraordinary!'

'It was an outrageous charge!' cried Rietti.

'Corvinus pleaded guilty to it,' said Obernyik simply.

'Under pressure of torture!'

'He has never retracted.'

'To whom would he retract? To you? What would it profit him, save further to increase the miseries and humiliations that have been heaped upon him throughout the years?'

'You puzzle me, Monsignor,' said Obernyik. 'Do you know that? You people of the Vatican, the high-ups of the Church. You made him a cardinal. Well, that was understandable enough. That red hat became a sort of martyr's crown – that would be the way you'd see it. Yet you have never made any real, hard attempt to secure his reprieve. Not in all those years. Not till now. Why is that?'

The pale hand that set down the sherry glass upon the desk top gave a slight tremor which was not lost upon the other man; and when Rietti answered, he did so without meeting the other's gaze.

'I think you are well aware of the reason, Mr Obernyik,' he said.

'You refer to the matter of the supper party. The photographs. Those unfortunate photographs. Ah, with what joy we sometimes enter into situations which we regret in the grey light of dawn.'

'It was – unfortunate,' said Rietti.

'It was more than that,' said Obernyik. 'For Corvinus to accept an invitation to a private supper party with Gauleiter Krantz and his friends was an act of professional *felo de se*.'

'A most unhappy circumstance,' said the Jesuit. 'Mark you, we are not convinced that His Eminence – Monsignor Corvinus as he then was – was involved in any impropriety. There was a little singing, so we understand. Though not of the religious sort.'

'Quite so,' said Obernyik. 'And was it necessary for Corvinus to sing with his arm wrapped round Gauleiter Krantz's neck? I refer you to photograph number seven in the set.'

'I have it here in the dossier,' murmured Rietti in a dying voice.

'And after the singing,' said Obernyik, with malicious persistence, 'the gipsy girls were brought in.'

'Those poor debauched women!' exclaimed the Jesuit. 'But here at least, Mr Obernyik, the finger of guilt cannot be pointed directly at His Eminence, who not only testified that he had departed for bed by that time . . .'

'Testimony that is fortuitously supported by the fact that he does not appear in the photographs that feature the women,' said Obernyik. 'However, he certainly left his biretta behind when he went to bed. It is to be seen upon the head of the commander of the Waffen SS Division Das Reich. I refer you to picture number eleven. The Obergruppenführer has a girl on each knee.'

'We have examined the entire set of photographs in detail,' breathed Rietti. 'And with much heart-searching.'

A great bell tolled the half-hour. Through the window, Obernyik saw a cloud of pigeons, disturbed by the sound, take off from a roof edge and swarm over the top of Michelangelo's dome. He had an impulse to laugh, but changed it to a discreet cough. He was really trying this poor cleric a long way, and he had further, yet, to take him.

'There was the question, also, of the housekeeper, was there not, Monsignor?' he asked blandly.

'All through the years, His Eminence's testimony . . .'

'He denied that there was cohabitation, yes.'

'So did the woman – at first,' said Rietti.

'Quite. It is a pity for Corvinus, however, that she afterwards emigrated to the United States, where she published a ghosted autobiography, which purported to tell, and in some wealth of detail, of her life with the handsome young cleric who became Cardinal Corvinus.'

'Is the word of such a creature to be trusted?' demanded Rietti with some asperity.

'Perhaps not,' conceded the other. 'And the more so after she moved to Southern California, had a sex change, and went through a form of marriage with a female tennis star. But her testimony remains to embarrass you, Monsignor. You and your Church are embarrassed. And all the red hats in the world will not quite cover your doubts about the egregious Corvinus. But now you want him back – why? To begin the rehabilitation?'

'Perhaps. And your people are willing to – as you say – extend a small mercy towards an old enemy?'

'There will be conditions, Monsignor.'

'Naturally.'

'My – superiors – are desirous that Rome should appoint an archbishop to the vacant see of our capital.'

'That is, surely, a very odd request for the leaders of an atheist state to make, Mr Obernyik. When one considers how His Eminence Cardinal Corvinus has been treated.'

'Times have changed, Monsignor,' replied Obernyik, with something of the embarrassment that the Jesuit had shown in an earlier part of their discourse. 'The possession of a prelate adds tone to one's seat of government, you understand. And what is good enough for Moscow is good enough for us.'

'I have full plenipotentiary powers to secure the return to Rome of His Eminence,' replied Rietti. 'You shall have your archbishop.'

'Then I think we are in business, Monsignor, and that speedy arrangements can be set afoot to have Corvinus escorted to Rome by air. To begin his – rehabilitation.'

Monsignor Rietti sighed and passed a frail hand across his pale, clever face.

'Time, and the opinion of men more charitable than we, will bring about His Eminence's rehabilitation. *Mutatis mutandis*,' he said. 'Mr Obernyik, you must not judge the whole Church on the evidence of your People's court proceedings against Cardinal Corvinus.'

'I do not, Monsignor,' replied Obernyik. 'Indeed, I do not. I judge by the best I find.'

By the intense look that he gave Rietti, a vainer man than the Jesuit might have thought that the Communist was alluding to him, and in this he would have been mistaken. Obernyik was thinking about the little nun at the street café – the one who had sparked off the most interesting discourse between himself and the Englishman with the missing hand.

Fernworthy arrived back at his hotel at around ten o'clock, by which time he had passed from the stage of being slightly maudlin drunk to being depressively near-sober. To his irritation, he found that his room key was not on the hook. The hall porter was away having his supper, and his assistant, a dull boy without a word of English, and a stutter to boot, was not able to account for the key's absence. Assuming that the chambermaid was perhaps up there turning back the coverlet, he went to his room.

The door was unlocked. Angela was sitting up in the middle of his bed, reading. She was wearing a black nightdress.

She put down the book.

'You take your bloody time, don't you?' she snapped.

THE ROOM PHONE rang at eight-thirty next morning. Fernworthy gave a guilty start when he heard the familiar harsh, slightly nasal drawl of Freddie Carruthers.

'That you, laddie? I'm speaking from Chiasso. Everything's fixed here. If all's right your end, we can do the job tomorrow.'

'Oh! Oh – I see.'

'You have fixed things your end?'

'Well . . .'

'Oh, for God's sake, laddie. There's so little for you to do in Rome, merely sighting out the land and deciding upon the venue – the combined telecommunications centre and dropping point for the merchandise. Don't tell me you didn't do that yesterday afternoon immediately you arrived. What have you been doing with yourselves – traipsing round bloody art galleries?'

'No – I – I've fixed the venue.'

'Where is it?'

'What?'

'I said, where is it?'

'It's a café,' said Fernworthy. 'Just – just like we agreed upon. It's – it's near to St Peter's Square and the Vatican. And to the hotel.'

'And it's got a telephone that's conveniently placed and private?'

'Er – yes.' Fernworthy bit his lip.

'You don't sound very sure. What's the name of this café and the number of the phone?'

'I – I can't remember.'

'You can't *remember*? Give me air! What kind of bloody fools am I mixed up with? Where's Angela? I tried her room first, but got no reply.'

'Oh! She – she probably went out. Yes, I remember now, she said she'd go out early and time the walk from here to the café. Just in case – you know – there's a traffic jam when we come to do the job, and we have to rely on walking.'

'That's good thinking at any rate. Thank God I can rely on her at least. All right, laddie. We're fixed at both ends, so it's on for tomorrow. I'll be in Rome this evening, along with the merchandise. What did you say?'

Fernworthy saw his own reflection in the mirror above the dressing-table – the table that was littered with unfamiliar items of womanly things: things like powder pots and eyebrow pencils, a wisp of blue chiffon. His expression looked like that of a little boy who has just been told that there is to be no Santa Claus this year.

'I – I thought you wouldn't be here till tomorrow at the earliest,' he said.

'No need for delay, laddie. Everything's cut and dried here. Besides – I'm missing the little wifie's ministrations. Nothing here in Chiasso that appeals to Freddie. See you this evening, boy.'

The phone went dead. Bastard! Bastard! Fernworthy slammed his fist against the wall. Why didn't I manage to kill the bastard that time? But I'll not bungle it next time. There must be a way . . .

He looked up to see that Angela had just come out of the bathroom and was standing and regarding him. The shower cap described the neat shape of her skull, and she had a towel looped round her hips. He swallowed hard.

'That was Freddie?' she asked.

'He's coming to Rome this evening.'

She shrugged. 'So?'

'You don't care?'

'Darling, we went to bed together last night, that's all. It wasn't the first act of *Tristan and Isolde*. Do I care that I've got to be pawed by that bastard just one more time? Yes, I do. But the sooner it's over and done with the better. Tomorrow, when I've got my share of the take, I'll be free. Free to fly to the uttermost ends of the earth and rid myself of Freddie Carruthers for ever. Always supposing that he doesn't double-cross us and make off with the lot – a thing that he will do with alacrity and a very real pleasure if we give him the slightest opportunity. Now, don't sulk. You don't please me when you sulk. And you really have such a marvellous face when it's in repose, darling. I quite fell for you the first time we met. You put me in mind of those early stills of John Barrymore. I was all in a flutter. Now, stop pouting, or you'll make me mad at you like I was yesterday in the Water Garden.'

'Why were you mad at me?' asked Fernworthy, reaching out for her.

'Because you started out by being direct and honest in your approach, then went all shifty and apologetic, like those horrid city businessmen with pouchy eyes and tobacco-stained moustaches who "accidentally" bump into one in crowded underground trains in the rush hour. So I ran away from you. Then I thought better of it.'

'Then you became direct and honest,' said Fernworthy. 'For which I was – and still am – profoundly grateful. Because, believe me, there, but for your honesty and directness, the whole thing would have foundered. And I would have gone celibate all the way to my grave.'

'That you will not do,' she declared. 'Not by a very, *very* wide margin . . .'

The café was called La Botella. They ordered breakfast there, at the same table where Fernworthy had sat the previous evening. He immediately made an anxious check on the telephone arrangements and found them to be excellent : three separate and virtually sound-proof cubicles, and easily accessible, with a view out into the street from all three. He reported as much to Angela.

'This is where it will all happen,' he said. 'Tomorrow we shall make a cool million here, in this very spot.'

'Does it make you anxious, nervous?' she asked.

'A little. And you?'

'Like I've told you, my only worry is that Freddie will do the dirty on us, like he did with me over the Spanish villas racket : walked away with the take and left me to face the rap. And, hell, I was young and innocent in those days; didn't even know that the villas were just a figment of an artist's imagination.'

The waiter brought coffee and rolls. Fernworthy waited till he had gone, and then he asked her the question that had long been nagging at a corner of his mind :

'Why did you marry him in the first place? As my father used to say, he's got cad written all over him.'

'Darling, don't you know that women – some women, young and romantically-inclined women – are crazy about cads and rotters? Such men seem so – dangerous. Like sleek and potent big cats. I used to think that Freddie was like some great tawny leopard. Actually, as I've learned to my cost, he's all rat.'

'How soon did you discover this?' said Fernworthy.

'On my wedding day,' said Angela. 'While I was changing into my honeymoon going-away costume, my husband of half an hour filled in the idle time by laying one of my bridesmaids.'

'Why didn't you leave him there and then?'

'I did. He came after me. Full of contrition. I forgave him.'

'And . . .?'

'He borrowed money from me to go down and pay off his taxi. I learned afterwards that he'd brought the bridesmaid with him in the taxi. Just in case the contrition scene fell flat. He always hedges his bet, does Freddie.'

'What a swine!'

She laid her hand over his. It felt very cool.

'Don't get exercised over him, darling,' she said. 'It makes you sound possessive, and I don't want to be possessed. Not even by a thoroughly nice person like yourself.'

'I'm not a nice person,' said Fernworthy. He took a deep breath and went on: 'I have a criminal mind. Indeed, I have been a practising criminal almost all of my life.'

'You are just trying to impress me, darling,' she said. 'You are trying to make like some great tawny leopard.'

Then he told her about the pickpocketing – he even called it by its proper name instead of the usual euphemism – about losing his hand on the job, everything. When he was done, he felt a whole lot better. Angela felt a whole lot worse; cried a little, and kissed him in full view of a passing pair of priests, who pretended not to notice.

That morning, they took a carriage and were driven round the Eternal City in the sunshine. He showed her the Forum Romanum and the Coliseum. At the foot of the Spanish Steps, he bought her flowers from the barrows with the big umbrellas, and they were pictured together, like bride and groom, by a street photographer. After a very boozy lunch at a restaurant on the Appian Way, they went back to the hotel. Freddie arrived in time for dinner, and so ended the first day of their love affair.

Freddie, playing the uxurious role to a sickening degree throughout dinner *à trois*, pawing at Angela's hand and offering her titbits from his plate, till Fernworthy all but brained him with an Asti Spumante bottle, turned sour and sullen when, she having retired to bed, and he having gone up after her, very soon returned and rejoined Fernworthy in the bar.

To Fernworthy's delight, he said: 'Never trust a woman, laddie. Barman, gimme a large dry martini, straight up and real dry. Yes, laddie. Take my case. That little wifie of mine, now she owes everything to me. Everything. Without me, she would have been nothing. A small-timer in an ad agency. Because of me, because I took her in hand, groomed her for the big-time, she transcended the mean and common lot for which nature and circumstance had designed her. Set up two more martinis, barman. You will join me, won't you, laddie? This is going to be a long night. Yes, laddie, a long night.'

I feel quite sorry for the poor bugger, thought Fernworthy. What a side-swipe for someone with his ego, to be locked out of his wife's room. You know, I may not find it necessary to kill him after all.

Not unless – not unless he tries to double-cross us, like Angela says he will, if he gets half a chance tomorrow . . .

JAY COKER HAD picked himself a hotel that was out of town and pleasantly situated so as to give him views of Lake Lugano, which he carefully described, supplementing the coloured photographs of the same, upon four identical postcards for Mrs Ducane and her offspring. Indeed, he nearly wrote a fifth; but checking with the date, decided that she had probably not yet been delivered of her latest blessing.

At nine o'clock precisely, and having partaken of a hearty breakfast of ham and eggs, coffee and rolls ad lib in the open-plan restaurant of the highly modern hotel, Coker stood by the telephone in his room and waited for a call from Freddie Carruthers. This, arriving dead on time, gave him the number of the middle one of the three call boxes in the café called La Botella in Rome. Armed with this last and vital item of information, the big American hefted his bag, checked out of the hotel, and drove a hired VW Beetle to a parking meter on the Corso San Gottardo in Chiasso and waited for the action to begin.

Chiasso, a frontier town, through which pass both main line rail and *autostrada* routes into Como and Milan, was busy that summer's morning. Coker sat at the wheel, the sunshine roof rolled back, chewing on a toothpick. Shops open early in Switzerland. Eight o'clock is the rule from Monday to Friday, and most banks are open before nine. A steady stream of new and well-kept automobiles paraded up and down past where Coker was situated, fifty yards from the door of the bank. He admired the good looks of the people in them. They went with the elegance of the lake, he thought, and with the wrinkled, violet-tinged crests of the mountains. Pretty soon, with the sun higher and more intense, the road surface began to steam and stink of gasoline and exhaust fumes, and Chiasso was like any place else.

At nine-thirty, checked by his wristwatch, an armoured truck of the security company rolled down the street and double-parked close by the bank entrance. Two heavyweights got out, menacing in crash helmets and protective truncheons, guns on hips. One of them spoke into a microphone on the side of the truck, and a canvas bag was delivered to the exterior through a sliding trap-door. One of the guards carried it swiftly through the door of the bank; his comrade accompanied him to the threshold, and stood there, glowering furiously at passers-by.

Coker uncoiled himself from the tiny car and strolled slowly down the sidewalk towards the bank door, where he passed under the angry scrutiny of the guard. He all but collided with the other as he came out, an action that almost cost him a blow on the head from a half-raised truncheon. Coker felt it in his heart to pity those two guys: with all that dough in their charge, they had cause to be nervous.

The banking hall was as busy as a city railroad station as Coker took up his place of observation at a desk that commanded an uninterrupted view of the last teller's booth in the line – the one that had been kept reserved, by prior arrangement, for the reception of the security delivery. The clerk behind the bullet-proof glass screen was busily counting out the high-denomination notes from the first of the canvas bags: United States 100 dollar bills and Swiss 1000 franc notes. The 'honest brokers' had been as co-operative as one could have wished, but had pleaded the impossibility of assembling the entire ransom, at such short notice, in the demanded dollars. So who's complaining about Swiss francs in this day and age?

Coker peered over the top of a sumptuously illustrated and suavely argued brochure on the advantages of the Swiss banking system, which he had taken from a rack on the desk, to see the helmeted thug re-enter with the second canvas bag. It had been determined, by the honest brokers, that the entire ransom could be contained in four bags. Four bags. One for each of us.

> One for you,
> One for me.
> One for you,
> One for you.

Taking two minutes each way from truck to teller's booth, the guard hefted the last bag through the bullet-proof screen at nine-forty, and allowed himself the relaxation of lifting his visor and lighting a cigarette. He had quite a wait in front of him: two million dollars takes a while to count, even in large denominations. He was well down a king-size coffin nail before the clerk had counted through the last bundle of notes.

Unnoticed and unsuspected, the big man in the T-shirt and jeans watched every move from the centre of the hall. He saw the clerk scribble his signature on a receipt slip and pass it to the guard, who put it into an envelope that he had taken from his tunic pocket. The guard then did a very curious thing – at least, he thought it was a curious thing to do, but those had been his instructions, and it was not for him to reason why: he slipped the envelope under a blotter pad that stood, together with a ballpoint on a chain, close by the teller's window. He then departed.

Coker swallowed hard. In all the deal, the next bit was the part he liked least. They had chewed it over, the four of them, far into the night on several occasions, but had never come up with anything better than the option upon which they had finally decided – which was simply to take the envelope from under the blotter pad and walk out of the bank.

He took several deep breaths, felt his adrenalin level mount to fight and flight capacity. Then, waiting till a small queue was beginning to form close by the scene of the action, he ducked quickly from behind a rather stout lady and gained the blotter pad, where he made to scribble a note upon the brochure he had taken from the rack. In the course of doing so, he slipped the envelope from under the pad.

The walk to the door was like the walk to the scaffold, every step an invitation to disaster. He died a thousand deaths, suffered a thousand indignities. Would it be the hand of a police detective that would fall upon his shoulder or that of a secret service operator? A bullet in the back from a KGB hit-man? A knife from a Red fanatic?

The automatic plate-glass door closed smoothly behind him and he stepped out into the sunlight. Quenching a temptation to run, he fixed his sight upon the VW and willed himself to think of absolutely nothing till he reached there. And the worse part was getting in and looking ahead along the downward-dropping bonnet, towards the bank.

He looked. No one appeared to have followed him out.

Over-revving wildly, Coker spun the wheel and sent the little car into a slot in the fast-moving, mid-morning traffic. He went for two blocks, then turned sharply down a one-way street of tall apartment houses; a quiet street, with just a few automobiles parked on meters, and not a soul in sight.

At the end of this street, he slowed to a halt and turned to look behind him. He was still looking ten minutes later, by which time, his heart was thudding from sheer joy and excitement.

He had not been followed. The honest brokers were what they had cracked themselves up to be. All they wanted was for the merchandise to be safely delivered.

He gave his *Alma Mater* yell.

Angela had been monopolizing the centre phone booth at La Botella since nine-thirty. Romans being of the easy-going sort, no one – particularly a male Roman – would have complained about a pretty woman hogging a public phone for so long. In the event, it was very quiet in the café that morning, and she had been the only telecommunicant.

From where he was sitting – at what he had come to regard as his usual table – Fernworthy could see the sleek, bowed top of her head as she mimed into the mouthpiece, her finger on the hook. He never heard the phone ring, and was not aware that she had taken the real call till her head bobbed out of sight. Moments later, she came out of the café door, and he knew by the wonder in her eyes that all had gone well.

'Gosh, I need a stiff drink after that,' she said.

'All's well?'

'Perfect,' she replied. 'You will be delighted to hear, darling, that our friends deposited the magnificent sum of two million US dollars into a numbered bank account – our bank account – in Chiasso at nine-thirty this morning, as arranged. Jay has the attested proof, bearing the number of the account.'

'We're nearly home and dry,' said Fernworthy.

'One small snag remains,' she said.

'What?'

'I can't get through to Freddie,' she said. 'I suppose the girl on the hotel switchboard's taking her coffee break.'

'Damn! It's just the sort of snag we envisaged,' said Fernworthy. 'And why we arranged this communication centre. Better try again in a few minutes, Angela.'

'I can do better than that,' she said. And in such a tight voice that he glanced at her sharply.

'What do you mean?' he asked.

'I don't trust that swine,' she said. 'Ed, I know – I just know – that he's going to double-cross us.'

'So what do you propose to do?'

She drained her glass and exhaled a long and shuttering breath.

'I duck out of the telephone job,' she said. 'Go to the hotel and pass the news on to him personally. Stick with him till he collects. Bring him back here.'

Their eyes met.

'Oh, for God's sake, darling!' she exclaimed. 'Don't tell me that you think I'm going to pull a double-cross on you as well!'

'It never occurred to me for an instant,' said Fernworthy. 'What did occur to me was that, if he really does intend to make off with the money, he might be dangerous. To you, I mean.'

She opened her handbag and held it out to him. With a start of alarm, Fernworthy saw the blue barrel of a little snub-nosed revolver, half-wrapped, in a nest of blue chiffon.

'And I'll use the gun if I have to,' said Angela. 'But believe me, Freddie will fold as soon as he sees it. For all the karate and the chest-beating, he doesn't have the guts of a weasel.'

'But you'll be careful?'

'Darling, I'll be so careful that it'll hurt.'

'And you'll come back here? Don't forget, I can't pass on the merchandise till I've heard that Freddie's collected.'

'I'll be back, like I told you. And with Freddie — even if I have to bring him here at gunpoint. 'Bye, darling. Keep cool.' She leaned forward and dropped a kiss on his cheek. Her perfume, her moist lips, hit his senses with a curious effect of *déjà vu*. He had an impulse to take hold of her, to keep her with him. Then she was gone; her dainty high heels click-clicking on the paving stones, her slim figure tall against the sunlight. It was ten minutes past ten.

Fernworthy ordered another coffee and brandy and settled down to wait. It would take Angela seven minutes to reach Freddie, who was stationed by the phone in his bedroom, waiting for her cryptic call: simply the number of the bank account, which would tell him that the money had been correctly paid over in Chiasso. Armed with that, he was scheduled then to go out to a safe phone box and contact the honest brokers, to arrange for the collection of the one thing that still remained: the authority which would permit them to draw the money. It had all been most carefully arranged. Freddie would be wild at her for quitting her post at the café. He would certainly realize that she was out to prevent him working a double-cross. Would the pistol be enough to protect her?

'God, I hope so!' he murmured aloud. And shifted uneasily in his chair.

The act of shifting brought the sole of his shoe in hard contact with some part of the contents of the large zipper hold-all that lay at his feet.

He looked down and shuddered: so close to the mute relics of World Revolution.

He had drunk too much, and too early. Not that it mattered. His remaining part in the plan was a mere delivery job, to be carried out on receipt of a signal. The effect of the brandy – which he normally never drank because it gave him palpitations – had been to sharpen his awareness.

He supposed that he was in love with Angela. It was a quite surprisingly pleasant sensation, and not entirely unfamiliar: he had experienced a similar set of responses from the occasional – and entirely fruitless – contact with a young woman who had occupied the flat below him before the Civil Service dragon had arrived. Back in the mists of time, there had been, also, a little girl named Millie at his nursery school. Strange, he thought, how one remembers . . .

What future, if any, for him and Angela? In the brief hours since their affair had begun, they had never touched upon a future for the relationship. Before and since, she had spoken only of escape. For her, the money was desirable only as the means to distance herself from the man to whom she was married. There had so far been no question of him, Fernworthy, playing any part of her flight to the uttermost ends of the earth.

This day – the day when, all being well, they would successfully pull off one of the biggest kidnapping coups in history – might well spell the end of it for Angela and him. It might be the unaccustomed morning brandy, but – strangely – he could not bring himself to feel despondent about the prospect. Was it because, some-where at the back of his mind, he did not believe that it was going to end? But that it would go on, and on . . .

Someone shuffled past him to sit at the table behind,

and in doing so clouted the back of his chair. Fern-worthy turned with a frown, and looked into a pair of dark eyes that flickered with pleased recognition.

'Why, good morning, it is you again.'

'Hallo,' said Fernworthy. 'How are you, Mr – er . . .?'

'Obernyik, Mr Fernworthy. An impossible name for an Englishman to remember, is it not? So you are sitting out here and making the most of the Roman sunshine, eh?'

'That's right,' said Fernworthy. 'I see in this morning's paper that they've got rain back in England.'

'Then you are lucky to be in Rome,' said Obernyik.

'If I'm lucky,' said Fernworthy feelingly. 'If I'm lucky, I shall be back in England tomorrow, with my business completed.'

'Ah, then, like me, you are not holidaymaking? That is interesting. I know you to be a man of education and perception. Might one enquire, Mr Fernworthy, what is your business?'

The arrival of the waiter for Obernyik's order absolved Fernworthy from the necessity of answering immediately. By the time Obernyik had requested a Cinzano and soda, he had assembled a cover story of sorts. As an improvisation, it had the virtue of being both mildly impressive and calculated to over-awe the casual enquirer into respectful silence.

'I work for my government,' said Fernworthy. 'And I am here on a special assignment.'

The dark, surely Magyar, eyes opened wide with astonishment.

'But that is a most amazing coincidence, Mr Fern-worthy,' he declared.

'Oh! Is it?' said Fernworthy, taken aback.

'Why, yes. I, too, am here in Rome on a special assignment. Not, I hasten to assure you, in connection with government service. I am – how to put it? – in travel agency.'

'How *very* interesting,' said Fernworthy fervently, letting his mind slide away to the contemplation of what might be taking place – he stole a glance at his watch – even at that very moment in Freddie's hotel room.

'Very exclusive travel agency, I hasten to add,' said Obernyik. 'Indeed, I am at present in Rome to facilitate the arrival of one single client.'

Fernworthy dragged himself away from his doleful speculations. Really, the fellow was most agreeable, with an extremely engaging manner. The sort of casual companion, if ever there was one, to divert one's thoughts for a brief while. He determined to let himself be diverted . . .

He said : 'Good heavens, Mr Obernyik, your client must be extraordinarily rich, to afford such exclusive service.'

'Not rich,' said Obernyik. 'Not as this world reckons riches. Indeed, for these many years, my client has been – greatly deprived. But he has very, very good connections in Rome.'

'Ah, and they are paying for his trip?'

'Oh yes, they will pay,' said Obernyik. The idea seemed to amuse him. 'But tell me, Mr Fernworthy – and please feel free to tell me to mind my own business – what, broadly, is the nature of your assignment here? In the most general and non-specific terms?'

Once again, Fernworthy was saved from immediately replying to a pointed question by the arrival of the waiter, this time with Obernyik's drink. In that brief reprieve, his mind flashed to the zipper hold-all close by his feet, and he determined to make some small sport – by way of a caprice, to pass the time – with his amiable companion.

When the waiter had departed, he said: 'To tell you the truth, Mr Obernyik, I am here in Rome to facilitate the removal, from our shores, of a fellow we shall be well rid of. And that's the truth of it. More than that I'm not at liberty to divulge.'

'A criminal?' asked the other.

'Thought by many to be an undesirable, certainly,' said Fernworthy. 'And a fornicator.'

Obernyik gave a harsh intake of breath, denoting disapproval.

'You may think me old-fashioned in my condemnation, Mr Fernworthy,' he said, 'but I cannot condone sexual misbehaviour. And I will confide in you, my friend, since you have been so frank with me, that my client . . .'

'The one whose arrival in Rome you are here to facilitate?'

'The very same. My client, in his youth, was a byword for the sort of behaviour you have mentioned. A fact that gives great pain to his influential connections here in Rome.'

'Yet, in spite of that, they are paying for him to have a holiday here?' asked Fernworthy.

'They make a habit – I might almost say a fetish – of forgiveness,' said Obernyik.

'It's a worthy quality, Mr Obernyik.'

'Indeed yes, my friend,' was the reply. 'But there are some who think that there is greater elegance in the principle of a transgressor getting his just deserts. And I am one of those.'

'I'm not so sure, Mr Obernyik, that I'm not of the same opinion,' declared Fernworthy, with Freddie Carruthers in mind.

'Then let us drink to that,' said Obernyik. 'May your fellow get his just deserts.'

'And your fellow also,' responded Fernworthy. 'In

fact, may they both suffer the fate they severally deserve.*

They touched glasses and drank.

'You laughed, Mr Fernworthy,' said Obernyik.

'I did not,' said Fernworthy. 'But someone did. I thought it was you.'

The other shrugged. 'We must have misheard,' he said.

They spent a brief time in silence, after which they fell to small talk, followed by more silence. For his part, Fernworthy had slipped away from the diversion provided by his companion's agreeable manner and had returned to black speculation about Angela. After some time, the man at the next table began to make small fussing movements of departure.

'It has been most agreeable, as before,' said Obernyik. 'But now I must go, for I have an appointment. Waiter!'

'Allow me to settle your bill,' said Fernworthy.

'I would not hear of it,' said the other, dropping a pile of coins in the plate. 'So pleasant to have made your acquaintance in Rome, Mr Fernworthy. Goodbye.'

Fernworthy did not return the valediction, indeed he did not see the departure of the Communist, for his attention was taken – and the sight set his heart going like a trip-hammer – by the approach of Freddie Carruthers, who was already swaggering down the street towards him; who had already seen him, and was giving a careless wave. He was grinning. He was also alone.

Freddie was wearing the lightweight hounds' tooth, double-breasted suit for which Fernworthy had provided the money as part of the operation. His tie was Harrow-side out, and he sported a green-tinged carnation in his buttonhole. The Mediterranean sun had done wonders for his habitually healthy tan, from out of which his perfect teeth gleamed whitely. He pulled out a chair and sat down beside Fernworthy.

'It's done, laddie,' he said.

Fernworthy said : 'Where's Angela ?'

'One thing at a time, dear boy,' said Freddie. 'Waiter, bring me a large scotch on the rocks and look sharp about it.'

'Damn you, where is she?' hissed Fernworthy.

Freddie grinned. 'Dear Angie, my little wifie, is not available to take nourishment at this point in time.'

'My God!' cried Fernworthy. 'If you've harmed a hair of her head, I'll . . .'

The other's eyes clouded with anger, then puzzlement, then amusement.

'Well, I'm damned!' declared Freddie. 'I do believe friend Fernworthy has been lusting after my little wifie all this time, the dirty old fox. By gum, I see it all. I suppose the pair of you are in it together. You knew she was coming round to the hotel to keep an eye on Freddie, to make sure he didn't abscond with the take. All that rubbish about no one answering the phone.'

'What have you done to her?'

Freddie's grin broadened. As the waiter laid his drink before him, he picked it up and took a deep swallow. Not till he had finished half the glassful did he carefully wipe his trim moustache with a red silk handkerchief and reply :

'As you had no doubt planned, the bitch pulled a gun on me. Unhappily for her, she was not quite quick enough for Freddie. I chopped her.'

'You did *what*?'

For answer, Freddie brought down the heel of his palm – quite lightly – upon the ashtray that lay at his elbow. The pottery saucer broke cleanly in half.

'Get the idea?' he said.

'Where is she?' breathed Fernworthy.

'Back at the hotel. I dumped her in her room. Don't get your knickers in a twist, Grandpa, she'll be up and about. But not for a little while. Folks whom Freddie chop stay chopped for quite some time.'

Fernworthy, by a concerted effort of will, forced himself to stop trembling. And, keeping the tremor from his voice as well as he was able, he said : 'Listen to me, Carruthers. I don't give a damn about your party tricks. Nor that you're a big beautiful bouncing boy, and I'm a middle-aged cripple. I promise you this : if you've hurt – really hurt – that girl, I'll kill you, so help me, if I have to wait a lifetime for the opportunity.'

Freddie's glance wavered. Disconcerted by the sheer vehemence and intensity of Fernworthy's outburst, his confident grin wavered at the edges.

'By jove, I reckon you mean that,' he said.

'You bet your life I mean it,' said Fernworthy.

'You're sweet on Angela ?'

'Yes.'

'She sweet on you ?'

'I don't know. I hope so. But I don't know.'

'Well,' said Freddie, raising an eyebrow, 'that puts a vastly different complexion on the situation. I came around here to put a proposition to you, but to you alone. If Angela and you have got a thing going, the deal's off.'

'What proposition – what deal ?' demanded Fernworthy.

Freddie had recovered his sang froid, and the objectionable grin was firmly back in place.

'I had in mind to split up the partnership,' he said. 'Unilaterally, of course. In short terms, I was going to cut you in, fifty-fifty, with the proceeds. In addition, we retain the merchandise and demand yet another pay-off from the Commies. I needed your assistance, you see, to work it again. Two of us could have done it second time round – now that we're familiar with the drill.'

'That is just about the dirtiest deal I can imagine,' said Fernworthy.

'Isn't it just, laddie?' admitted Freddie cheerfully. 'I really am a cad through and through, aren't I? I was born rotten.'

'I'll settle for the straight pay-off,' said Fernworthy. 'And I speak for the other two. You will divvy-up four ways, as arranged.'

The other shook his head. 'No deal, laddie. Freddie takes all.'

From his breast pocket he produced what looked like an elaborate credit card. It bore the famous name of the bank in Chiasso, and was embossed with a code number.

'So that's it?' said Fernworthy, with a touch of awe that reflected his feelings at the sight of the card. 'The thing we've worked for and dreamed of!'

'Our honest brokers delivered it on request,' said Freddie. 'I phoned them from a phone box as soon as I'd dealt with Angela. They played square, just like they did in Chiasso. No fooling, no tricks. Half an hour ago, as I instructed, this guy descends the Spanish Steps and lays the card on the balustrade half-way down. As instructed, he looks neither left nor right, nor behind him, but proceeds straight across the piazza and heads for the Tiber. Freddie picks up the card. End of story.'

'And now you propose to keep it for yourself,' said Fernworthy flatly.

'With this card,' said Freddie, 'with this card, dear boy, I can open the door of my private Aladdin's cave in every city in the world that contains a branch of the bank. This number you see embossed here – which, incidentally, checks out with the one that Coker phoned from Chiasso – is the key to two million beautiful dollars which Freddie is going to spend all on his very own. Sorry, laddie, I would have made a deal with you over trying to squeeze another payment from the Commies, but I'm not cutting Angela in as well. You can keep the merchandise and try your luck.'

'Thanks,' said Fernworthy.

'My pleasure, laddie. Regard it as a wedding present from me – assuming that you and Angie are contemplating a spot of bigamy. And now I must be going.'

I should kill him now, thought Fernworthy. For what he's done to Angela, back there in the hotel. For cheating us like this. But most of all for what he might have done to her. If he's smashed her face. That face . . .

Freddie drained his glass and got to his feet, shot his cuffs, straightened his Old Harrovian tie, smoothed down his glossy hair, flicked the ends of his moustache.

'Cheerio, laddie,' he drawled. 'Take my tip and get yourself fixed up with a false hand. That stump looks quite gruesome, and I'm sure it must turn Angie off.'

'I prefer it this way,' growled Fernworthy. 'And so does Angela.'

'Each to his taste,' said Freddie. 'Pip pip, laddie.'

He set off across the road, and had gone three paces from the kerb, when Fernworthy called out to him:

'*Freddie! You've dropped the bank card!*'

Freddie halted. Looked down. One hand flew to his breast pocket, fumbled there for an instant. Emerged with the card. He flashed a grin and frowned with mock disapproval.

'Naughty old Fernworthy,' he said. 'Trying to put the wind up poor Freddie.'

A woman screamed.

Next instant, the flying motor-bus hit the elegantly-suited figure and slammed it in the air like a broken doll; catching it again with a shattering of windscreen glass; pounding it beneath fat tyres.

Another woman was screaming. People were running from all sides. Most of them slowed down when they saw the state of what had once been Freddie Carruthers.

Fernworthy nerved himself to walk over to the twitching body, arriving there at the same time as a policeman. The latter was so busy trying not to throw up that he never noticed the bank card lying close to one scrabbling hand with its carefully shot shirt-cuff. Fernworthy had his foot on the card in a trice, and it was in his pocket by the time the policeman had covered the worst of the body with his tunic.

'He went the same way as his father,' said Fernworthy. 'Run over, just like his dear old dad. I'm sure he wouldn't have wished to go any other way.'

'*Mi scusi, signor?*' said the policeman.

'Nothing, Officer. Nothing at all.'

The ambulance had taken the remains. The fire engine had come and washed down the street. Most of the people had drifted away. It was nearing lunch-time, and the café tables were filling up with a fresh clientele who had come for their apéritifs and had no inkling of the tragedy that had been staged there such a brief time before.

Fernworthy picked up the zipper hold-all and took it inside the café, to the centre phone box. There, he dialled a Rome number. The receiver at the other end was snatched up at the first ring.

'Yes? Who is that?' It was the voice of the fellow he had contacted first in London.

'It's me,' said Fernworthy.

'I'll have the code words first, mister.'

' "It is true that liberty is precious – so precious . . ." '

'Okay, okay. What now? We've done everything you ordered. Are you going to fulfil your part of the bargain?'

'Yes. Did you think we wouldn't?' asked Fernworthy.

'I never had any doubts about you, but I didn't like the sound of your mate. The guy with the phoney, cut-glass accent and the bad manners.'

'He's much improved now,' said Fernworthy. 'In fact, he's changed out of all recognition. Listen, the merchandise is in a telephone box. The middle one of three inside the café called La Botella, which is in the via di Porta Angelica, close by the Vatican. There will be an "out of order" sticker on the door of the box, which should keep the merchandise safe for a while but not for ever. So you'd better make it snappy.'

'La Botella. Via di Porta Angelica. I'll be right over.'

Fernworthy replaced the receiver, tucked the zipper hold-all as far out of sight as possible and went out, closing the door of the booth behind him and, after a swift glance round to make sure he was unnoticed, sticking a prepared label on the glass door: *NON FUNZIONA PIU*.

He had emerged into the street, when an odd recollection struck him, and so forcibly that it brought him to a halt. It had happened in the box, while he was stooping down to push the hold-all against the wall. He had seen something, and registered it on his eyes' retina almost unconsciously. It must have been a trick of the light, a reflection from the glass walls. Or, again, perhaps he had imagined it. But for a brief instant he had seemed to see a printed word on the side of the hold-all, where no word should have been. Very odd, and quite absurd.

At that moment, a taxi came rattling down the street, and it was free. He flagged it down and got in, giving the driver the name of his hotel, and asking him to go as fast as possible.

All through the journey, he nagged himself with worry about Angela, and what state he might find her in. Only once did he have a brief respite from his anxieties about her : this was when something clicked into place in his bank of memory, and he seemed to assemble the word – the entirely imaginary word – that he had certainly *not* been printed upon the hold-all.

The word was – *Aeroflot.*

Marcia Funèbre

I

OBERNYIK WAS kept waiting for nearly an hour and missed his lunch. The Monsignor, so he was informed by the severe cleric in the outer office, had been summoned, and here the speaker nodded to the Papal Apartments, whose high roof loomed above the Bernini colonnades at the far side of St Peter's Square. Obernyik fell to wondering if Rietti got on as badly with his chief as he, Obernyik, did with his.

After a while, the intercom gave a squawk.

'Has Signor Obernyik arrived?'

'Yes, Monsignor.'

'Send him in, please.'

The severe cleric motioned the visitor to the door, which he held open for him. Rietti, who must have entered his office by another way, was washing his hands in a basin at the far end. He greeted Obernyik without turning, then splashed his face with water and reached for a towel.

'This intolerable Roman summer heat,' he said. 'One perspires so badly. Do take a seat, my dear Obernyik.' Curiously vulnerable-looking without their spectacles, his short-sighted eyes peered vaguely in the other's direction. 'Tell me, how is the matter progressing? Have your superiors agreed to our agenda?'

'They have done better than that,' replied Obernyik. 'In fact, I may say that, as far as our side is concerned, the matter is completed.'

'Completed? You don't mean . . .'

Wordlessly, Obernyik lifted the bag that stood at his feet — it was a large zipper hold-all — and placed it on top of the Jesuit's desk. Rietti, who had hastily affixed his half-moon spectacles, gazed upon it in awe.

Presently, he found his voice. 'Is *that* — but surely it cannot be — His Eminence?'

'It is,' said Obernyik.

'But there seems — so little of him.'

The Communist shrugged. 'A man brings nothing into the world, and leaves precious little behind him when he is gone. You will find all of your cardinal here, Monsignor Rietti. I am informed that the bones were exhumed from the prison graveyard yesterday.'

'Ten years,' breathed Rietti. He crossed himself. 'Ten years in unconsecrated ground.'

Obernyik looked affronted. 'That is as may be,' he replied. 'But I hasten to assure you that Corvinus received the best of all possible medical care during his last illness. The personal physician of the head of state attended him. A specialist was summoned, even, from Moscow. The sanctity of life, even the life of an enemy of the People, is respected by us, atheists though we be.'

'I am sure this is so, my dear Obernyik,' said Rietti hastily. 'I am *quite* sure this is so. Believe me, we are most grateful, most grateful, for your co-operation in the matter of returning His Eminence to a last resting place in St Peter's. You must all have taken a tremendous amount of trouble with him,' he added.

'He was brought by scheduled Aeroflot flight,' said Obernyik. 'In charge of a courier from our Foreign Office. I, myself, collected him at Leonardo da Vinci this morning, and . . .'

He fell silent. Stared intently at the hold-all

'My dear Obernyik!' exclaimed Rietti. 'Whatever is the matter? Why are you acting in that alarming manner? Is something troubling you, pray?'

The Communist's hands reached hesitantly towards the hold-all. Then it seemed that he feared to touch it, and his arms fell to his side.

'Speak to me, Mr Obernyik, I beseech you!' pleaded the Jesuit.

'It can't be true,' whispered Obernyik.

'*What* can't be true?' wailed Rietti.

'I could swear – I see it in my mind's eye quite plainly,' said Obernyik. 'When I took the bag from the courier at the airport, I noticed that is was an extra-large-sized airline bag, with the word *Aeroflot* printed on the side, in Roman – not Cyrillic – lettering you understand, such as the Russians use for many purposes on their international schedules. AND THIS BAG IS QUITE PLAIN!'

The Jesuit transferred his horrified gaze to the hold-all, peering closely at it through the thick lenses of his glasses, at close quarters.

'I see no lettering here,' he said. 'Mr Obernyik, you are not telling me that . . . ?'

'I never let it out of my sight for an instant,' said the Communist. 'From the moment I took it from the courier and signed his delivery note, to the moment when I walked into this room.'

'Did you – call anywhere on the way?'

'At a café, merely, to kill half an hour,' said Obernyik dismissively. 'The bag I placed by the side of my seat, and took it up immediately upon leaving.'

The Jesuit's unaccommodating face sketched the outlines of a wintry smile. 'Well then, my dear Obernyik,' he said. 'Since all other probabilities are ruled out, there remains only one option: you were mistaken in your first observation. You saw lettering on a bag at the airport, perhaps on many bags. But not on *that* bag.' And he folded his arms and looked wise.

'There is only one way to settle the matter,' said Obernyik.

'There is, indeed,' agreed Rietti.

Slowly, the Communist reached out for the tag of the zipper. Paused. Drew it slowly back. A glance at the pale face of the Jesuit, and he looked inside. Instantly, his countenance was washed clean of alarm. He gave a sigh of utter relief.

'His – Eminence is there?' asked Rietti.

Obernyik nodded. 'See for yourself, Monsignor.'

Rietti did so . . .

'What a blessing, indeed, Mr Obernyik,' he declared. He swallowed hard, and his prominent Adam's apple jounced up and down. 'If there had been any mistake, if, for the sake of argument, you had *mislaid* His Eminence, I tremble to think of the repercussions that might have emanated from – ' he glanced out of the window, across St Peter's Square – 'or the disastrous result it could have had upon my career – my vocation.'

Obernyik spread his hands. 'For me, it would have been a short walk and a bullet in the back of the neck,' he said.

'Would you care for a glass of sherry, Mr Obernyik?'

'Do you have anything stronger, Monsignor?'

'I keep a little cognac for emergencies.'

'This, Monsignor, is an emergency.'

Angela was slumped across the bed in her hotel room. There was a dark bruise across her right temple, and she had been crying. She looked up when he entered.

'Oh, thank God it's you,' she murmured, when he put his arms about her.

'Are you all right?'

'He knocked me out cold,' she said. 'The bastard's quicker than I thought. More cunning than I'd remembered. He never turned a hair when I went into his room. All smiles. Fooled me completely. Not till I'd given him the number of the bank account did he show by word or gesture that he knew I'd come to prevent him from double-crossing us. I remember half pulling the gun from my bag. Next moment, everything went black.'

'Don't worry,' said Fernworthy. 'Everything's all right.'

'I feel so weak and helpless,' she cried. 'I came round a little while ago, and all I could do was sob like a baby. Darling, I'm afraid we've lost out. He's picked up the bank card, and we aren't ever going to set eyes on it.'

'How about this then?' murmured Fernworthy. And he took out the card and showed it to her.

Wide-eyed, she met his gaze.

'Darling, how did you get it off him?' she breathed.

'Later,' said Fernworthy. 'I'll tell you later. Right now, we're checking out and flying back to London to join Jay Coker.'

'But – where's Freddie?'

'I'll tell you about that over a drink on the plane. Now, pack your things. I'll ring for a porter to carry our bags down, and I'll meet you in the hall.'

She clung to him.

'Ed, darling,' she breathed against his cheek, 'I don't know how you've done it, but you've done it. And you're wonderful. Wonderful!'

'That's me. See you downstairs.'

He patted her cheek and walked out. His own room was four doors down. He unlocked it and went in, to find the place in semi-darkness. Why ever did the chambermaid draw the blinds? He crossed over to the window, and the door clicked behind him. He drew back the blind, and turned to see three men regarding him in the sweep of sunlight that flooded the room.

'Hallo, mister. We meet at last.'

The speaker was seated in an armchair. He was a thin-faced Latin in his mid-forties. Clever-looking, with a humorous twist to the corners of his mouth. Dressed in a discreet black lightweight suit, white shirt, knitted silk tie, Gucci shoes. Fernworthy recognized his voice as as soon as the first syllable came over.

' "It is true that liberty is precious . . ." ' said Fernworthy, feeling foolish as he uttered the quotation.

The other smiled, showing a row of gold inlays. 'No need for identification when face to face, Mr Fernworthy,' he said. 'We have known you by sight for — quite a while.'

There was a tap at the door, and the handle revolved.

Instantly, the other two men – big, silent, taciturn men – produced automatic pistols from their hips.

'Darling, the door's locked. Can I come in?' It was Angela.

Fernworthy looked – as much for guidance as any-thing – to the man in the chair. With a terse economy of gesture, the Latin advised him what to do, pointing sharply to the door, then drawing a finger savagely across his throat.

Fernworthy swallowed, and called out: 'I – I'm just taking a quick shower, darling. Do you mind? See you down in the hall.'

'All right,' came her reply. 'Tell you what . . .'

'What?'

'That's the first time you've addressed me as darling. Do you know that?'

'Is it?'

'It is. And it could be the subject for further discourse. See you downstairs.'

Silence. The man in the chair smiled his quirky smile again. The big men by the door tucked their automatics back in their waistbelts and leaned back against the wall, arms folded.

'The Southern Italian Communist Party appears to be very well-organized,' said Fernworthy, for the sake of something to say.

The other smiled his golden smile. 'When we speak of Southern Italy, we refer, specifically, to Sicily,' he said. 'Sicily is our place of origin, but we have branches everywhere: London, Rome, Chicago, Las Vegas, you name it. And, though not strictly Communists, we live by that best of all Communist principles: "What's yours is ours". Perhaps you have heard of us.'

'I have heard of you,' said Fernworthy.

'Take a seat, Mr Fernworthy,' said the other, pointing. 'Do you know that I am a great admirer of yours? We have had a dossier on you ever since you extended your pickpocketing activities beyond the place where you went to school – Uppingham, was it not? And such a pity about young Mr Arthur Ealing's tragic end; you made a great pair of operators. I put up the proposition to my principals that you be admitted into our Society. You could have been of tremendous assistance in some of our political operations. What treasures of indiscretion you might have picked up at diplomatic soirees in Washington, garden parties at Buckingham Palace, and in the lobbies of the United Nations building. Regrettably, the proposition was shelved, and now it is too late.' His button-bright dark eyes fell compassionately upon Fernworthy's stump.

'Great heavens!' exclaimed Fernworthy.

'You are surprised,' said the other. 'It is not to be wondered at. The extent of our activities, though wildly exaggerated in some areas, is greatly under-estimated in others.'

'How soon did you find out we had taken – the merchandise?' asked Fernworthy.

'Now, there I have to compliment you, Mr Fernworthy. The kidnapping was brilliant. Originally conceived, imaginative in execution. It had style. Real style. And that is praise indeed, I assure you, coming from us. We have been into the kidnapping scene for generations. We practically invented it.'

'Thank you,' said Fernworthy.

'Am I correct in my assumption that the germ of the plan – the interior plot, so to speak – emanated from your good self?'

'That is so,' admitted Fernworthy.

'I thought as much. It has your style.∎

'Again – thank you.'

'As to the pick-up, however –' the other demonstrated his viewpoint with another mime: pinching his nose between finger and thumb – 'the whole thing stank from beginning to end. Your ingenuousness in accepting us, without checking our credentials, in our self-styled role of honest brokers. The interminable – and easily traceable – telephone calls. Oh yes, we even have our methods of tracing calls. But, most of all, the pick-up at Chiasso, and again at the Spanish Steps. *Incapace!* Really, it was like dealing with the rankest amateurs – which is, indeed, what you are. And that is not to detract, Mr Fernworthy, from your former role as a master dip.'

One of the gunmen against the wall unwrapped a stick

of chewing gum and stuck it in his mouth. A bell struck in a nearby campanile.

'What happens now?' asked Fernworthy, whose stomach was tying itself in knots, and whose hand was clammy with dread.

'First – the bank card,' said the other. 'The two million dollars is ours. Working capital to secure the merchandise. It was, of course, out of the question for us to bother with collecting those paltry sums from all and sundry all over the globe. The card, Mr Fernworthy.' He held out his hand.

Numbly, Fernworthy took the precious rectangle of plastic from his pocket and laid it on the table within reach of the other's hand. It remained there, untouched.

'What else?' asked Fernworthy.

'Now we eliminate you,' was the bland reply. 'And then the woman. And then Mr Coker.'

'Oh, my God!'

'It is regrettable, but necessary. We do not like – loose ends lying around. Loose ends, from our experience, tend to unravel a whole operation. And we have far to go with the merchandise with which you so kindly provided us.'

'Not the others!' pleaded Fernworthy. 'Kill me if you must, but not the others. Not – her.'

There was very real sympathy in those dark Latin eyes. And a lot of admiration.

'Ah, yes, the beautiful Mrs Carruthers. One gathers from the conversation through the door that your action in disposing of her husband was not entirely motivated by business considerations. The disposal, by the way, was beautifully staged. I have received a report on it. The simulated accident is the most difficult of all hit-jobs to perform. Your timing was masterly.'

'It wasn't intended!' exclaimed Fernworthy. 'At least — I don't know. I saw the bus coming. But I don't know . . .'

'You have very quick reflexes, my friend. Almost subliminal. It is a quality, of course, that made you into such a superb pickpocket.'

Dimly, as if through smoked glass, Fernworthy saw the glimmer of an opportunity presenting itself. He sought for words to put it into a coherent shape.

'Er, Signor – er . . .'

'Benny,' said the other. 'Just call me Benny, as all my friends do.'

'What I was going to say was – er, Benny – that I should be very happy to offer my services to the – er – Society, as a hit-man. Specializing in the simulated accident. In return for our lives.'

Benny shook his head. 'I am very sorry, Mr Fernworthy,' he said. 'But we have all the hit-men we can use. In any event, your chances of duplicating that hit and getting away with it are thousands to one. Disregarding that, you do not have the physical equipment for a hit-man, just as you do not have the physical equipment to be a pickpocket any longer.'

'Is there nothing I can do, Benny?'

'To save her? She is that much to you, Mr Fernworthy?'

Fernworthy nodded. 'Yes.'

'You would kill, even?'

'I think so. Yes, I think I would kill. To save her.'

'I believe you,' said Benny. 'Everything we have on file about you suggests that you are a man of tremendous basic integrity. Passionately loyal. Ruthless. Ruthless, even, to the point of self-sacrifice. Correct?'

'I don't know,' admitted Fernworthy. 'I only know that I would do anything to save Angela. And, of course, that has to include poor old Jay.'

Benny eased himself more comfortably in the chair. Crossed his legs. Examined the toe of one of his elegant Gucci shoes. His shrewd face was pensive. Fernworthy experienced a small *frisson* of hope.

'I am thinking,' said Benny, 'that we could perhaps do a deal. As to your terms – freedom for Mrs Carruthers and Mr Coker?'

'That's right. And . . .'

'Yes?'

'Can they retain the bank card? I mean – after all, what's two million dollars to your Society?'

'It is chicken-feed, Mr Fernworthy,' said the other frankly. 'Small change. Picayune. A drop in the ocean. Contemptible. But, Mr Fernworthy, there is a principle involved. *We* are not in business to give, but to receive. Charity is not our *métier*. Kindness – okay. Kindness – a little kindness now and again – that costs nothing. Once a society like our gets into charity, it could become expensive.'

'Those would be my terms, Benny,' said Fernworthy with as much firmness as he could muster – and it was not a lot. 'Spare their lives and let them have the card. After all, we provided you with the merchandise, so it's a straight sale and in no way offensive to your strong principles regarding the evils of charity. Moreover, I presume you're intending to make much more than two million on the operation.'

The other threw back his head and laughed, showing that his back molars were all of gold. When he had recovered his composure, he said : 'More than two million? I should say we are going to make more than two million, my friend. We shall not fritter the merchandise away on the first comers, as you were willing to do. We shall hold on to it and wait for the market to rise. Our experts in this type of merchandise tell us that moves in the relics market have become fiercely unpredictable . . .'

He rambled on. It's going to be all right, thought Fernworthy. This chap's basically on my side, and we'll make a deal. Angela and Jay will have their lives and the cash. I'll make the best of whatever they make me go through with. What's he going on about now?

Benny said: 'Take my home village, Mr Fernworthy. The poorest piece of farming land in all Sicily, yet the folks are prosperous. Have been for centuries. Me, I went to an expensive seminary. My sister, she married a notary. And you know how come all this prosperity? We got ourselves a relic in the church. A finger bone. The finger bone of a minor saint no one ever heard of. But this bone is special: *it moved once!* Just once! This was vouched for by the poor parish priest, who died the richest priest in the province. For ever since that day, the folks have come from far and wide to our village, to be there when that finger bone moves again. Meanwhile, everyone in the village is into the tourist racket – only we call them pilgrims and charge them double for everything. You talk about two million for a whole skeleton. Mr Fernworthy, the folks of my village wouldn't let that single old finger bone go for two million!'

'So they can have the bank card?' asked Fernworthy.

Benny shrugged. 'Okay.'

'And what do I have to do?'

'You take the rap for a murder. Get sentenced to life. Do maybe – oh – four or five years in a model prison and get paroled.'

Fernworthy flinched. 'Who – who's going to be murdered?' he asked. 'And when?'

'A very bad-type guy who won't be missed,' said Benny. 'And he already was. Rubbed out, I mean. By chance, he was rubbed out the afternoon you arrived in Rome. That's what makes it such a sweet set-up.'

II

THE PRISON WAS on the Adriatic coast. From the window of the chapel where Fernworthy was working, he
could see the ships coming and going, to and from
Venice, Trieste, Pula; dots in the shimmering blueness,
with chalk lines drawn out behind them.

He got down from the staging set against the altar
wall and, standing well back, narrowed his eyes and
inspected the mural he was painting. It was coming
along pretty well. The subject was the Marriage at
Caana, which has been done to death by the old masters,
but still offers opportunities for a new approach. He had
it in modern dress, and the wedding feast was taking
place at a long table set outside the café called La
Botella in the via di Porta Angelica. He had had a lot
of trouble with the figure of Christ, but the arrival of a
new young warder named Officer Croce had solved all
his problems. Croce, with his Northern Italian fairness
and blueness of eye, was the epitome of Our Lord as
idealized by Latins. The wedding guests were all the
people he had known best in his life. The red-headed
boy eating a pizza was Arthur Ealing as he had been at
school. The waiter with the bowl of spaghetti was Jay
Coker. Delicacy had restrained him from picturing
Freddie Carruthers; but the Virgin was – who else? –
Angela.

Not bad for a month's work with the left hand. In the
years that lay in front of him, he would have time to
paint murals over the entire interior, including the
underside of the tiny dome. Scenes from the New Testa-
ment, interpreted in the Italy of today, with likenesses

of the people he knew, the people all about him: the Governor, the Chief Warder, Guiseppi, with whom he shared a room – they weren't called cells in this model prison. Guiseppi was a lifer, too, and would make a splendid Judas Iscariot.

A step in the porch. The screen door swung open.

'Visitors for you. Better look sharp.'

'Coming, Officer Croce.'

'It's going well, the painting.'

'It hasn't looked back since I had you for a model, Officer Croce.'

He descended the steps from the chapel and crossed the formal garden. Guiseppi straightened up from pruning a rose bush and waved across at him.

'You got your first visitors, eh?'

'That's right.'

'One of them's a bird.' Guiseppi sketched an hour-glass shape and winked evilly.

'I know.' Yes, definitely Judas Iscariot for Guiseppi.

The reception block was a long, low building in the modern style, and it discreetly announced a note of humane restraint. The windows were large and un-barred; but were of bullet-proof thickness, like those in the rest of the prison. There were no locks on the doors; but one passed through an electronic scanner at every portal. Activated by the special strip of metal that was sewn into the seam of Fernworthy's trousers, the mechanism gave a gentle buzz as he entered, and the officer at the reception desk looked up.

'Number three booth, Fernworthy. You have ten minutes.'

'Thank you, Officer.'

The booth had a seat facing a glass screen through which there was no contact other than sight. His heart leapt to see Angela's face framed there, with Jay Coker at her shoulder.

'Darling, how are you?' She was trying very hard not to cry.

'You're sure looking fine, Ed,' said Coker. Both their voices came to him, quite clearly, through stereophonic speakers.

'I'm feeling fine,' said Fernworthy. 'This place is just like a holiday camp.' She was in a summery dress, with a bandeau as she often favoured. He had never seen her looking lovelier, and he supposed she had made a special effort for him.

She was biting her lip; looking at him in the way that told him she was the bearer of what she believed to be bad news.

'Darling,' she said. 'Steel yourself for bad news. They've refused your appeal.'

'No grounds for a retrial,' said Coker. 'Man, that frame-up sure sewed you up real good.'

'It's what I expected,' said Fernworthy, and hoped they would leave it at that.

They didn't . . .

'Darling, who could have *done* it to you?' said Angela. 'It must have been one of the Communist organizations, don't you think? Maybe even the KGB. The very brutality of it. Gunning down that crooked politician and then setting it up to look as if you had done it after we parted company in Tivoli that afternoon. How could they have found out so much about your comings and goings? And then to have got hold of your wristwatch without your knowing and putting it in the murdered man's hand. It was – diabolical! Oh, Ed darling . . .'

'Take it easy, babe,' said Coker gently, putting an arm about her shoulder and nodding conspiratorially at Fernworthy.

'What are you up to these days, Jay?' asked Fernworthy smartly.

'I'm glad you asked me that, comrade,' replied the
big American, who was certainly looking very prosperous in a hand-sewn lightweight suit and a velvet
bow tie the size of a windmill. 'I am just about to set
off on a world tour. This is in aid of the project I told
you about.'

'The home for people in need of help?'

'Right. I aim to find me a part of the world with
the largest percentage of folks like Eunice, and that's
where I'll build me my home.'

'How is Mrs Ducane, Jay?'

'Great! I got her off my hands at last. She's gonna
marry Sid. Sid's the tally-man and the father of her
latest, which is triplets, would you believe. Ain't that
nice? Well, he can't really marry her. He's married
already. So's she. But it's nice for the kids to have a male
around the house. Gives stability, you know what I
mean?'

'How are you getting along with the bank card?'
asked Fernworthy.

'Like a dream, man,' said Coker. 'Me, I've withdrawn
my share and deposited it in another bank, leaving the
card for you and Angela. Look, I'll leave you two alone
now. So long, Ed. I wanna say it's been great knowing
you, and it ain't over yet. I'll visit you right after I get
back from the trip. And when you get your parole, Ed,
we're gonna have great times. Yes, sir. Great times.' The
big American's voice was throaty, and he looked away,
rubbing his nose vigorously.

'See you, Jay,' said Fernworthy, as the expensively-
suited giant shambled away down the corridor beyond.

They were alone . . .

She raised a hand and placed it against the glass. He

did likewise, his palm facing her palm; the small hand entirely obliterated by his.

'It won't be long,' he said.

'It will be an eternity,' she contradicted. 'But we shall survive it.'

'Now that I've been here a month,' he said, 'I can have visitors every week. Shall you come and see me sometimes?'

She smiled. 'I bet you're asking all the girls.'

'But of course. I've come on a lot since I met you.'

'I'll think about it,' she said. 'In fact, quite by chance, I've taken a villa down there by the shore. It's very grand.'

'I love beautiful women, and I love rich women. But rich, beautiful women are best.'

'I know you're only after my money.'

'Of course. That's why I married you.'

He took away his hand, uncovering hers. The left hand, with the plain gold band that they had let him place there, in the Romanesque basilica behind the courthouse, after the trial and sentence, with two escorting prison warders as witnesses.

'I'd hoped you'd buy yourself an engagement ring,' he said. 'You'll have to get it yourself, for the prison shop's fresh out of engagement rings with stones the size of pigeons' eggs.'

'All my life,' she said, 'I've been surrounded by chaps who bought me simple things. Things like one perfect rose, one modest spray of fuscia. At last I've got a man who buys me a simple diamond ring the size of pigeons' eggs. Darling, I'm missing you.'

The door opened behind him.

'Time up, Fernworthy.'

'Thank you, Officer.' He turned, and deliberately let his eyes slip out of focus so that he should not see the whole of the glory in her eyes and be left inconsolable.

'Till next week.'

'Till next week.'

He turned on his heel, and went out of the booth without looking back.

He was not in the mood for more painting, and the rules of the establishment allowed the prisoners either to pursue a hobby in the evening, congregate in the TV room, or spend the time before supper in their rooms. Fernworthy decided he needed solitude, and having ensured himself that Guiseppi was still immersed in his beloved roses, he went to their room.

Like the rest of the prison, the room-blocks were spacious, airy, light. A single bed at each end of the room, a toilet and shower to every five rooms. No locks on the doors, but the ubiquitous electronic scanner transmitted a buzz to a central control panel in the guard block every time an inmate went in or out.

Fernworthy threw himself down on his bed, arms pillowed behind his head.

It was all over, yet in a sense it had only just begun. The next part was waiting time, and that wouldn't be so bad. Angela would come to him every week. When he started picking up privileges – and he meant to become a model prisoner – they would be able to meet for as long as an hour at a time, with no intervening glass screen. But that would come later.

Meanwhile, there was the world of the mind : the memories of the past weeks with Angela, the images of their future.

And present consolations . . .

The rule of the establishment allowed long-term prisoners to hang a modest number of pictures in their rooms. Guiseppi had a photo of his mother in a frame that he had made by glueing matchsticks together. Next door to that was his second choice: a naked woman cut out of what is known as a middling hard porn girlie magazine.

Fernworthy let his gaze wander slowly and luxuriantly over to the Boudin that hung on the wall opposite his bed; to the calm of the long-gone summer's morning on the beach at Trouville, with the crinolines, the parasol, the little white dog, the bright splash of the tricolour. And he wept for love and joy.

The new purveyors of the merchandise took their time over the disposal. Piece by piece, and at grossly inflated prices, the relics were vended throughout the world. In remote communes by paddy fields, in People's Palaces of Rest and Culture, in Temples of the Proletariat uncounted, fragments of Cardinal Corvinus were, by the strange turns of mischance that have been recorded here – brought to final resting places undreamed of by that worldly and dubious Prince of the Church. Meantime, back in the Eternal City, Requiem High Masses were sung for His Eminence, and the time-honoured expertise of the Congregation of Sacred Rites brought to bear upon the rehabilitation of the Cardinal's reputation, both worldly and spiritual. Meantime, his supposed remains were laid to rest within the walls of St Peter's, and a simple bronze tablet set to mark the spot.

And down the eternal corridors of time and space there echoed a peal of unearthly laughter.